START

START

5 Minute Stories

This edition published by Parragon Books Ltd in 2014

Parragon Books Ltd
Chartist House
15–17 Trim Street
Bath BA1 1HA, UK
www.parragon.com

Designed by Claire Brisley, and Kait Eaton at Duck Egg Blue
Edited by Laura Baker and Catherine Ard
Production by Charlotte McKillop

ISBN 978-1-4723-5210-1

Printed in China

5 Minute Stories

Parragon

Bath • New York • Cologne • Melbourne • Delhi
Hong Kong • Shenzhen • Singapore • Amsterdam

Contents

Aladdin

Once upon a time, a boy called Aladdin lived with his mother. They were so poor that every day it was a struggle to find enough money for food.

One day a man came to their shack saying he was Aladdin's long-lost uncle. When he said he would help Aladdin to make his fortune, Aladdin and his mother were delighted.

Aladdin travelled with him into the desert until they came to a rock. The man pushed it aside, revealing a hidden cave.

"You must climb down into this cave and fetch a lamp that you will find there," he said. "Bring it to me. Don't touch anything except the lamp. Wear this magic ring to protect you."

Aladdin was afraid, but he dared not argue with his uncle. He put on the magic ring and climbed into the cave. As soon as he was through the entrance his eyes grew wide with wonder. All around, piles of gold and jewels stretched from floor to ceiling. Gemstones glittered in the dim light. Just one ruby would make Aladdin and his mother rich. But he did as he had promised and touched nothing. At last he found a dull, brass lamp.

"Surely this can't be it?" Aladdin thought, but he took it back to his uncle. When he got to the opening, he found he couldn't climb out of the cave holding the lamp.

"Pass it to me," his uncle said, "then I will help you out."

"Help me out first, uncle," Aladdin replied, "and then I will give you the lamp."

"No!" the man shouted. "First give me the lamp!"

When Aladdin refused, the man became angry. He rolled the stone over the opening to the cave, trapping Aladdin in the dark.

"Uncle!" Aladdin shouted. "Let me out!"

"Hah!" the man shouted back. "I'm not your uncle, fool! I'm a sorcerer! You can stay there and die, if you won't give me the lamp!"

Aladdin wrung his hands in despair. As he did so, he rubbed the magic ring the sorcerer had given him for protection. Suddenly, a genie sprang out.

"I am the genie of the ring. What do you require, oh master?" The genie bowed. Aladdin was astonished, but he thought quickly.

"Please take me home to my mother," he said. And immediately he was outside his mother's house. He told her everything that had happened, and she hugged him with relief.

"Oh, but Aladdin," she cried, "we are still poor!"

The next day, Aladdin looked at the lamp he had fetched from the cave. "It doesn't look like much," he thought, and he started to polish it, hoping he could sell it to get money for food. As soon as he rubbed the lamp, another genie appeared.

"I am the genie of the lamp. What do you require, oh lord?" the genie asked. This time, Aladdin knew what to do. He asked the genie to bring food and money so that he and his mother could live in comfort.

Life went on happily, until one day Aladdin saw the beautiful daughter of the emperor. He fell in love and felt that he couldn't live without her. But how could he marry a princess?

Aladdin thought and thought, and finally he had an idea. He asked the genie for beautiful gifts to give to the princess.

When the princess spoke to Aladdin to thank him for the gifts, she fell in love with him. They were married, and Aladdin asked the genie to build them a beautiful palace.

Hearing that a wealthy stranger had married the princess, the sorcerer guessed that Aladdin must have escaped from the cave with the lamp.

One day, when Aladdin was out, the sorcerer disguised himself as a poor tradesman. He stood outside the palace calling out, "New lamps for old! New lamps for old!"

Aladdin's wife remembered the ugly brass lamp that Aladdin kept and took it to the man. The sorcerer snatched it from her, rubbed the lamp and commanded the genie to carry the palace and the princess far away to his own home in another country.

"Where is my beautiful wife?" cried Aladdin when he returned home, wringing his hands in despair. As he did so, he rubbed the ring and the first genie appeared.

"What do you require, master?" the genie of the ring asked.

"Please bring back my wife and palace!" Aladdin pleaded. But the genie of the ring was less powerful than the genie of the lamp.

"Then take me to her so that I can win her back!" Aladdin said.

At once, he found himself in a strange city, but outside his own palace. Through a window he saw his wife crying, and the sorcerer sleeping. Furious, Aladdin climbed in through a window and crept to the bedroom. He slipped the magic lamp from beneath the sorcerer's pillow and rubbed it.

"What do you require, master?" asked the genie.

"Take us straight back home," Aladdin said. "And shut this sorcerer in the cave for a thousand years – that will teach him a lesson!"

In a moment, the palace was back where it belonged. With the sorcerer gone, Aladdin and the princess were safe again. They lived long and happy lives together and never needed to call on the genie again.

The End

The Little Red Hen

There was once a little red hen who lived on a farm with her friends: a sleepy cat, a lazy pig and a stuck-up duck.

One day, the little red hen was scratching around in the farmyard when she found some grains of wheat. She was just about to peck them up when she stopped and thought.

"If I plant these grains of wheat instead of eating them," she said to herself, "they will grow tall and strong and make more wheat!" So she tucked the grains of wheat into her apron and went to see her friends.

"Who will help me to plant these grains of wheat?" she asked.

The cat opened one eye.

"Not I," she said. "I'm too tired."

"Not I," snorted the pig. "It's far too hot to work."

"Not I," quacked the duck, and stood on one foot.

So the little red hen found a patch of soil. She moved the stones and dug the earth. She made a row of holes and planted all the grains of wheat. Then she watered them carefully and left them to grow.

All summer, the sun shone on the grains of wheat and the rain fell on them. Each day, the little red hen checked they were not too dry or too wet. She pulled up the weeds and made sure the wheat had space to grow. At last, the wheat was strong and tall with fat, golden grains.

"This wheat is ready to harvest," she said to herself. "That will be a lot of work." The little red hen went to see her friends.

"I have worked all summer and the wheat is ready. Who will help me to harvest it?" she asked.

The cat stretched lazily.

"Not I," she said. "It's time for my nap."

"Not I," snorted the pig. "I need to roll in the mud."

"Not I," quacked the duck, and she preened her feathers.

So the little red hen took her tools and went to harvest the wheat. She cut down the wheat stalks and piled them up neatly. When she had finished, she went back to her friends.

"I have worked all day to cut down the wheat," she said. "Who will help me to make it ready for the mill?"

The cat yawned.

"Not I," she said. "I'm sleepy."

"Not I," snorted the pig. "I'm going to lie in the sun."

"Not I," quacked the duck, and tucked her head under her wing.

So the little red hen went back to the field alone. She beat the wheat to free the grains from the stalks, and carried away the straw. The wind blew, and the little red hen worked long and hard. At last, she swept up the wheat and put it into a sack. She carried it back to her friends.

"I have worked all day to prepare the wheat," she said. "Who will help me to carry it to the mill?"

"Not I," said the cat. "I need a rest."

"Not I," snorted the pig. "It looks far too heavy."

"Not I," quacked the duck, and she waddled away to the pond.

So the little red hen carried the heavy sack of wheat all the way to the mill. The kind miller ground the wheat to flour and poured it back into the sack. Then the little red hen carried it all the way home again.

The little red hen was exhausted.

"I have carried the wheat to the mill and had it ground to flour," she said. "Who will help me to bake it into bread?"

"Not I," said the cat, and she curled up, ready to sleep.

"Not I," snorted the pig. "It's nearly time for my dinner."

"Not I," quacked the duck, and she sat on the ground.

So the little red hen made the flour into dough and kneaded it. She shaped it into a loaf and put it in the oven to bake. After a while, a delicious smell wafted from the kitchen. The sleepy cat opened her eyes. The lazy pig came to stand by the oven. The stuck-up duck waddled in.

At last, the bread was cooked. The little red hen carried the loaf to the table. It had a beautiful golden crust on the top and was creamy white inside. It smelled wonderful.

"Who will help me to eat this loaf of bread?" the little red hen asked quietly.

"I will!" said the sleepy cat, washing her paws with her tongue.

"I will!" grunted the lazy pig, licking his lips.

"I will!" quacked the stuck-up duck, flapping her wings.

"No, you will not!" the little red hen said. "I planted the grains and watched them grow. I harvested the wheat and took it to the mill. I ground the flour and baked the bread. My chicks and I will eat the loaf!"

And that is what they did. The little red hen and her little chicks ate up every crumb of the hot, fresh bread.

The End

Goldilocks and the Three Bears

Once upon a time, there was a little girl called Goldilocks, who had beautiful golden hair. She lived in a pretty house right at the edge of the forest. Each morning she liked to play outside before breakfast, gathering flowers and looking at the animals who lived in the trees.

One day she strayed further than usual. She skipped happily along the forest path, chasing butterflies, until she was far from home and very hungry.

Just as she was thinking that it would take a long time to walk back for breakfast, a delicious smell wafted through the wood. She followed it all the way to a little cottage.

"I wonder who lives here," Goldilocks said to herself. "Perhaps they would share their breakfast with me?" She knocked on the door, but there was no answer.

As Goldilocks pushed gently on the door, it swung open. The house inside was cosy and inviting. Even though she knew she shouldn't, Goldilocks stepped inside.

The delicious smell was coming from three bowls of steaming porridge on the table. There was a great big bowl, a middle-sized bowl and a teeny-tiny bowl. Goldilocks was so hungry that – even though she knew she shouldn't – she tasted the porridge in the biggest bowl.

"Ew!" she cried. "This porridge is too hot!"

Next, she tasted the porridge in the middle-sized bowl. "Yuk!" she said. "This porridge is far too cold!"

So finally she tried the porridge in the teeny-tiny bowl.

"Yum!" Goldilocks said. "This porridge is just right!" And she ate it all up.

With her tummy nice and full, Goldilocks decided to have a rest before she set out for home. She looked around the room for somewhere to sit. There were three chairs, a great big chair, a middle-sized chair and a teeny-tiny chair.

She climbed onto the great big chair.

"This chair is far too high," she said.

Next, she tried the middle-sized chair, but she sank deep into the cushions.

"No," she said, "this chair is far too squashy."

So she sat on the teeny-tiny chair.

"This chair is just right!" she said, settling down. But Goldilocks was very full of porridge, and too heavy for the teeny-tiny chair. It squeaked and creaked. It creaked and cracked. Then...

Crash!

It broke into teeny-tiny pieces, and Goldilocks fell to the floor.

"Well, that wasn't a very good chair!" she said crossly. Then, even though she knew she shouldn't, she went to look upstairs.

In the bedroom were three beds. A great big bed, a middle-sized bed and a teeny-tiny bed.

She tried to lie down on the great big bed, but it wasn't at all comfy.

"This bed is too hard and lumpy," she grumbled. Then Goldilocks lay down on the middle-sized bed, but that was no better.

"This bed is too soft and squishy," she mumbled. And so at last she snuggled down in the teeny-tiny bed.

"This bed is just right!" she said, and fell fast asleep.

Now, whenever there is a house with porridge and chairs and beds, there is usually someone who lives there, and that was true of this house. Three big brown bears lived there: a great big daddy bear, a middle-sized mummy bear, and a teeny-tiny baby bear.

The three bears had made their porridge and gone out for a walk in the woods while it cooled down. At last, they went home for their breakfast.

"Why is the door open?" Daddy Bear said, in his deep, gruff voice.

"Why are there footprints on the floor?" Mummy Bear said, in her soft, low voice.

Baby Bear said nothing.

They went over to the table and Daddy Bear looked in his bowl.

"Someone's been eating my porridge!" he growled.

Mummy Bear looked in her bowl.

"Someone's been eating my porridge!" she exclaimed.

Baby Bear looked in his bowl.

"Someone's been eating my porridge – and they've eaten it all up!" he cried in his teeny-tiny voice.

Daddy Bear stomped over to his chair.

"Someone's been sitting in my chair!" he growled. "There's a long hair on it!"

"Someone's been sitting in my chair!" Mummy Bear exclaimed. "The cushions are all squashed!"

Baby Bear looked at his chair.

"Someone's been sitting in my chair," he cried, "and they've broken it into pieces!"

"Let's get to the bottom of this," Daddy Bear growled, and they padded upstairs to the bedroom.

Daddy Bear saw the rumpled covers of his bed.

"Someone's been sleeping in my bed!" he grumbled.

Mummy Bear saw the jumbled pillows on her bed.

"Someone's been sleeping in my bed!" she said.

Baby Bear padded up to his bed.

"Someone's been sleeping in my bed – and they're still there!" he cried.

The three bears crowded around the sleeping girl. Baby Bear reached out a fuzzy paw to touch her golden curls.

Goldilocks opened her eyes. Imagine her surprise when she saw three bears peering down at her! She leapt out of the bed, ran down the stairs, through the door, along the path and all the way home. And she never visited the house of the three bears ever again.

The End

Puss in Boots

There was once an old miller who had three sons. When the miller died, he left the mill to his oldest son. The middle son was given the donkeys. The youngest son, a kind man who had always put his father and brothers before himself, was left nothing but his father's cat.

"What will become of me?" said the young miller's son with a sigh, looking at his cat.

"Buy me a fine pair of boots and I will help you make your fortune, for your father thought you deserved it," replied the cat.

A talking cat! The miller's son could not believe his ears.

So the miller's son bought the cat a fine pair of boots and the two of them set off to seek their fortune.

After a while they came to a grand palace.

"Wouldn't it be wonderful to live so grandly," said the miller's son.

Later, while the miller's son was sleeping, the cat went hunting and caught a rabbit. He put it in a sack and took it to the palace.

"A gift to the king from my master, the Marquis of Carabas," said the cat, presenting it to the king.

The cat went back to the miller's son and told him what he had done.

"Now the king will want to know who the Marquis of Carabas is," laughed the cat.

A clever cat! The miller's son could not believe his ears.

Every day for a week, the cat delivered a gift to the king, each time saying it was from the Marquis of Carabas. After a while, the king became very curious and decided he'd like his daughter to meet this mysterious nobleman, whoever he might be.

When the cat heard that the king and his daughter were on their way, he wasted no time.

"You must take off all your clothes and stand in the river," the cat told his master.

The puzzled miller's son did as he was told and the cat hid his master's tattered old clothes behind a rock.

When the cat heard the king's carriage approaching, he jumped onto the road and begged for help.

"Your gracious majesty," said the cat, "my master was robbed of all his clothes while he was bathing in the river."

The king gave the miller's son a suit of fine clothes to wear.

"Please join us in the carriage," said the king.

So the cat opened the door and the miller's son climbed in. He looked very handsome in his new suit. The king's daughter fell in love with him at once.

The cat ran on, cutting through the surrounding countryside. Every time he met people working in the fields, he told them, "If the king stops to ask who owns this land, you must tell him it belongs to the Marquis of Carabas."

Beyond the fields, the cat reached a grand castle. He spoke to the people working in a field next to it and discovered that it belonged to a fierce ogre. The cat stood bravely in his boots and knocked on the castle door.

"Who dares to disturb me?" roared a voice from inside the castle.

"I have heard that you are a very clever ogre," called the cat. "I have come to see what tricks you can do."

The ogre opened the door and immediately changed himself into a great snarling lion. The cat felt scared, but he didn't show it.

"That is quite a clever trick," said the cat, "but a lion is a very large creature. I think it would be a much better trick to change into something very small, like a mouse."

The ogre liked to show off his tricks. He changed at once into a little mouse. The cat pounced on the mouse and ate him up.

Then the cat went into the castle and told all of the servants that their new master was the Marquis of Carabas. They were glad to be rid of the fierce ogre, so they did not complain.

"The king is on his way to visit, and you must prepare a grand feast to welcome him," said the cat.

When the king's carriage arrived at the castle, the cat was waiting to welcome him.

"Your gracious majesty," he purred, "welcome to the home of my master, the Marquis of Carabas."

A cunning cat! The miller's son could not believe his eyes.

"You must ask for the princess's hand in marriage," whispered the cunning cat to his master.

The miller's son did as he was told.

The king, who was impressed by everything he saw, agreed.

Soon, the Marquis of Carabas and his wife were married and they lived a very happy life together. The cat was made a lord of their court and was given the most splendid clothes, which he wore proudly along with those fine boots that the miller's son had bought him.

The End

Rapunzel

Once upon a time, a young couple lived in a cottage beside a stone wall. They were very poor, but very happy as the woman was expecting a baby. On the other side of the wall lived an old witch. The witch grew many herbs and vegetables in her garden, but she kept them all for herself.

One day the couple had only a few potatoes to eat for their supper. They thought of the wonderful vegetable patch on the other side of the wall. It was full of delicious-looking carrots, cabbages and tomatoes.

"Surely it wouldn't matter if we took just a few vegetables," said the wife, gazing longingly over the wall.

"We could make such good soup," agreed her husband.

So the young man quickly climbed over the wall and started to fill his basket with vegetables.

Suddenly he heard an angry voice.

"How dare you steal my vegetables!" It was the witch.

"Please don't hurt me," begged the young man. "My wife is going to have a baby soon!"

"You may keep the vegetables – and your life," she croaked. "But you must give me the baby when it is born." Terrified, the man had to agree.

Months later, the woman gave birth to a little girl. Immediately, the witch arrived and grabbed the child. Though the parents begged and cried, the cruel witch took the baby. She called her Rapunzel.

Years passed and Rapunzel grew up to be kind and beautiful. The witch was so afraid of losing her that she built a tall tower with no door and only one window. She planted thorn bushes all around it, then she locked Rapunzel in the tower and never let her see anyone else.

Each day, Rapunzel brushed and combed her long, golden locks.

And each day the witch came to visit her, standing at the foot of the tower and calling out, "Rapunzel, Rapunzel, let down your hair."

Rapunzel hung her hair out of the window and the witch climbed up it to sit and talk with her. But Rapunzel was very lonely. She longed to leave the tower and to make friends her own age. Each day, she sat at her window and sang sadly.

One day, a young prince rode by and heard beautiful singing coming from the witch's garden. He hid behind a thorn bush, hoping to see the singer. But instead he saw the witch. He watched as she stood below the tower and called, "Rapunzel, Rapunzel, let down your hair."

The prince saw the cascade of golden hair fall from the window and he watched the witch climb up it.

He waited until the witch climbed back down the hair and returned to her house. Rapunzel began her song again.

Enchanted by Rapunzel's lovely voice, the prince climbed over the wall and crept to the tower.

"Rapunzel, Rapunzel, let down your hair," he called softly.

Rapunzel let down her locks and the prince climbed up.

Poor Rapunzel was terribly afraid – she had never seen anyone except the witch before. When the prince explained that he only wanted to be her friend, Rapunzel was delighted. From then on, the prince came to visit her every day. Each time, he carefully waited until after the witch's visit before calling to Rapunzel to let down her hair.

Months passed and Rapunzel and the prince fell in love.

"How can we be together?" Rapunzel cried. "The witch will never let me go."

The prince had an idea. He brought silk which Rapunzel knotted together to make a ladder so that she could escape from the tower.

One day, without thinking, Rapunzel remarked to the witch, "It's much harder to pull you up than the prince!"

The witch was furious!

"Prince?" she shouted. "What prince?"

The witch grabbed Rapunzel's long hair and cut it off. Then she used her magic to send Rapunzel far into the forest. The girl made her home amongst the animals and birds, and sang sadly as she collected fruit and berries to eat.

Soon, the prince came to the tower and called,

"Rapunzel, Rapunzel, let down your hair."

The witch held the golden hair out of the window and the prince climbed up and up and into the tower.

But instead of Rapunzel, he came face to face with the ugly old witch.

"You!" screamed the witch. "You dare to visit Rapunzel? You will never see her again!" And she pushed the prince back out of the window. He fell down and down, right into the thorn bushes below. The sharp spikes scratched the prince's eyes and blinded him. Weeping, he stumbled away.

After months of wandering, blind and lost, the prince heard beautiful, sad singing floating through the woods. He recognized Rapunzel's voice immediately and called out to her.

Rapunzel ran to the prince and held him in her arms.

"At last, I have found you!" she said, and cried with happiness. As her tears fell onto his hurt eyes, the wounds healed, and the prince could see again.

"My love!" he said, and kissed Rapunzel.

Rapunzel had never been so happy. She and the prince were soon married, and Rapunzel's parents came to the wedding. Rapunzel and the prince lived happily ever after in a grand castle, far away from the old witch and her empty tower.

The End

The Three Little Pigs

Once upon a time, three little pigs lived together with their mother. As they grew bigger, their small house became too crowded. So at last she sent them off into the world to seek their fortunes.

"Be careful," she said. "Here, you are safe from the big, bad wolf. But out there, you will need to build strong houses."

The pigs set off happily. After a short time, the first little pig met a farmer pulling a cartload of straw.

"Please may I have some straw to build a house?" the little pig asked.

"Certainly," the farmer said, "but it won't make a very strong house."

The little pig didn't listen. He took the bundles of straw and stacked them up to make a house. When it was finished, he went inside for a rest.

Soon, the big, bad wolf came down the road. He hadn't eaten all day. When he saw the new house of straw, his tummy rumbled and he licked his lips.

"I smell piggy," he said to himself. "Yum!"

He peeked in through the window.

"Little pig, little pig, let me come in," he growled.

"No way!" the pig shouted. "Not by the hairs on my chinny-chin-chin!"

"Well, this house doesn't look very strong," the wolf said.

"I'll huff and I'll puff, and I'll blow your house down!"

So he huffed and he puffed, and he blew the house down. Straw flew everywhere, and the little pig ran away as fast as he could.

The second little pig walked a little further. At last he came across a woodcutter with a pile of sticks.

"Please could I have some sticks to build a house?" the little pig asked.

"Certainly," said the woodcutter. "Take as many as you like, but they won't make a very strong house."

The second little pig didn't listen. He picked up all the sticks he could carry and took them to a clearing. He piled them up to make a cosy house. When it was finished, he went inside and settled down with a cup of tea.

The big, bad wolf was cross and hungry. When he saw the house of sticks, his tummy grumbled and he licked his lips.

"I smell piggy," he said to himself. "Yum, yum!"

He pushed his nose against the door.

"Little pig, little pig, let me come in," he growled.

"No way!" the second little pig shouted. "Not by the hairs on my chinny-chin-chin!"

"Well, this house doesn't look very strong," the wolf said.

"I'll huff and I'll puff,
and I'll blow your house down!"

And so he huffed and he puffed, and he blew the house down. The sticks tumbled to the ground, and the little pig ran away as fast as he could.

The third little pig walked further still, until he saw a builder with a pile of bricks. The builder was just finishing work.

"Please could I have some bricks to build a little house?" the third little pig asked.

"Certainly," the builder said. "Those are left over. Take as many as you want."

So the third little pig carried the bricks away and built a beautiful house. When he had finished, he went inside, put a pot of water on the fire and started to make some soup.

After a while, his two brothers came running up the path.

"Let us in!" they shouted. "There's a big, bad wolf coming!" The third little pig quickly let them in. They locked and bolted the door and sat down to wait.

Before long, the big, bad wolf came huffing and puffing up the path. When he saw the new brick house, his tummy rumbled and grumbled and he licked his lips.

"I smell piggy – and soup!" he said to himself. "Yum, yum, yum!"

He knocked hard on the door.

"Little pig, little pig, let me come in!" he roared.

"No way!" the third little pig shouted. "Not by the hairs on my chinny-chin-chin!"

"Well, then," the wolf said,

"I'll huff and I'll puff,

and I'll blow your house down!"

And so he huffed and he puffed, and he huffed and he puffed... but the house stood firm.

The wolf looked up and saw the chimney. He climbed onto the roof, and down the chimney he went – straight into the pot of hot soup.

"Owwwwooooooo!"

He jumped out of the pan and ran yowling and howling out into the cool night. The big, bad wolf ran up the path, over the hills and far away, never to be seen again. The three little pigs lived happily ever after, all together in the strong brick house.

The End

Pinocchio

There was once a carpenter called Geppetto. One day, he was walking through an enchanted forest when he heard a voice.

"Hello," it said.

Geppetto looked around, and soon realized that the voice was coming from a magic piece of wood.

"Talking wood," he thought. "How unusual!"

Geppetto took the magic wood home and carved a little puppet boy from it. He gave the boy a suit of clothes and a hat with a feather in it. The wooden boy danced around the room for Geppetto and made him laugh. "Hello!" he said.

Geppetto named the boy Pinocchio.

"You must go to school like other children," Geppetto told him.

So the next morning, Pinocchio skipped off to school on his wooden legs.

As he went along, a cricket hopped up onto his shoulder.

"You look like you could use a friend," he told Pinocchio. "I will help you to learn right from wrong."

A little further down the road, Pinocchio met a fox and a cat. They had heard the sound of dinner money jingling in his pocket.

"Don't bother going to school," said the fox. "Come and play with us instead!"

Pinocchio, not knowing any better, thought that sounded like a good idea.

"I don't think you are doing the right thing," the cricket told him. "You promised your father you would go to school."

But Pinocchio paid no attention to the cricket.

The cat and the fox led Pinocchio into a dark forest. "If you plant money here, it will grow into a money tree," they told him. "Just come back tomorrow, and you'll see."

"That doesn't sound right," said the cricket. "That money was for your dinner."

But Pinocchio didn't listen. He dug a hole in the ground and buried the coins in it.

Then Pinocchio went home, feeling very hungry. He did not tell his father that he hadn't been to school.

The next morning, Pinocchio didn't go to school either. Instead, with the cricket on his shoulder, he skipped into the forest to find his money tree.

When Pinocchio reached the spot where he'd buried his coins, there was no money tree. He dug down to look for the coins he had planted, but they were gone.

"The fox and the cat have played a trick on you," said the cricket. "They just wanted to get your money."

Pinocchio felt rather silly, but he pretended he didn't care. He stomped off into the forest.

"I'm going on an adventure," he said.

The little cricket begged him to go back to Geppetto, but Pinocchio walked on until it was dark and he was a little scared.

Soon they came to a tiny cottage. Pinocchio ran to the door and knocked loudly. A pretty fairy with turquoise hair answered the door.

"We're lost," explained Pinocchio. "Please can you help us?" The fairy invited them in and gave them some food.

"Why are you so far from home?" she asked kindly.

Pinocchio did not want to tell her that he had disobeyed his father.

"I was chased by a giant!" he lied.

Suddenly, Pinocchio's nose grew a little.

"The giant was taller than the trees..." continued Pinocchio.

Pinocchio's nose grew some more.

"And I ran into the forest to escape!" he continued.

And Pinocchio's nose grew again!

He touched it in wonder.

"I have put a spell on you!" said the fairy. "Every time you tell a lie, your wooden nose will grow."

Pinocchio began to cry. How he wished he had gone to school like his father had said!

"I won't tell any more lies," promised Pinocchio.

The fairy called some friendly woodpeckers who pecked at Pinocchio's long nose until it was back to the way it used to be.

In the morning, Pinocchio rushed back through the forest with the little cricket perched on his shoulder.

"From now on I will do just as Father tells me," he said. But when he got home, Geppetto wasn't there. Instead, there was a note on the kitchen table.

> Dear Pinocchio,
> I have gone to look for you. I miss you, my son.
> Your loving father, Geppetto.

Pinocchio was very sad. He knew he had caused a lot of trouble.

"We must find my father and bring him home," he sobbed. So he and the cricket set off again at once.

They began their search down by the river. Pinocchio stood too near the edge of the water, and he fell in with a SPLASH! The cricket jumped in to help him, but they were both swallowed by an enormous fish.

There, in the fish's tummy, they found Geppetto!

Pinocchio hugged his father tightly. "I won't leave you again!" he said.

The clever wooden boy took the feather from his hat and tickled the fish.

"A...a...a...tishooo!" The fish gave a mighty sneeze and Geppetto, Pinocchio and the cricket shot back out through the fish's mouth and landed on the bank of the river.

That night, when Pinocchio was tucked up in his own little bed fast asleep, the fairy with turquoise hair flew in through his window.

"You are a good, brave boy," she said as he slept. And she kissed him on the forehead.

When Pinocchio awoke the next morning, he found that he was no longer made from wood. He was a real boy! From then on he was always a good son to Geppetto and the best of friends with the cricket, who didn't need to tell him right from wrong ever again.

The End

The Lion and the Mouse

Once upon a time, there was a huge lion who lived in a dark, rocky den in the middle of the jungle. When the lion wasn't out hunting, he loved to curl up in his den and sleep. In fact, as his friends knew, if he didn't get enough sleep, the lion became extremely grumpy.

One day, while the lion lay sleeping as usual, a little mouse thought he'd take a short cut straight through the lion's den. The mouse lived with his family in a hollow at the bottom of a tall tree just on the other side of the lion's rocky home. He was on his way home for supper and didn't want to have to climb up and over the big boulders surrounding the den.

"What harm can it do?" he thought. "He's snoring so loudly, he'll never hear me."

As he hurried past the snoring beast, he accidentally ran over the lion's paw. With a mighty roar, the lion woke up and grabbed the little mouse in one quick motion.

"How dare you wake me up!" the lion roared angrily. "Don't you know who I am? I am King of the Beasts! No one disturbs my sleep. I will kill you and eat you for my supper." He opened his huge mouth wide.

Shaking with fear at the sight of all the lion's sharp, pointed teeth, the terrified little mouse begged the angry lion to let him go.

"Please, Your Majesty," he cried. "I didn't mean to wake you up. It was an accident. I was just trying to get home to my family. I'm too small to make a good meal for someone as mighty as you. Let me go and I promise to help you one day."

The grumpy lion stared at the little mouse. Then he laughed loudly.

"You help me?" he said scornfully, shaking his furry mane. "Ha! Ha! Ha! What a ridiculous idea! You're too small to help someone as big as me."

The little mouse trembled and closed his eyes as he waited for the terrible jaws to snap him up.

But to his surprise, the lion didn't eat him. Instead, the lion smiled and opened his paw.

"Go home, little mouse," said the lion. "You have made me laugh and put me in a good mood, so I will let you go. But hurry, before I change my mind."

The little mouse was very grateful. "Thank you, Your Majesty!" he squeaked. "I promise to be your friend forever, and I won't disturb you again."

As quickly as he could, the little mouse scurried home. What a story he would have to tell his children!

A few days later, the lion was out hunting in the jungle. As he crept stealthily through the lush undergrowth, he smelt something delicious. There, in a small clearing just ahead of him, stood a goat, eating the grass beneath a shady tree.

The lion circled the clearing, slowly crawling through the tall grass. He crouched low, ready to pounce on the unsuspecting goat… when suddenly a big net fell on him.

He was trapped in a hunter's snare!

The goat, bleating in terror, ran off into the jungle. The lion roared and tried to break free from the trap. But the more he struggled, the more he became tangled in the net. He was so angry that he let out the loudest of roars.

RROOAARR!

The trees in the jungle shook with the terrible noise. Every animal for miles heard it, including the little mouse.

"Oh no!" squeaked the mouse. "That's my friend, the lion. He must be in trouble! I've got to go and help him."

"Be careful, my dear," cried the mouse's wife. "Remember how big he is!"

The little mouse scurried through the jungle as fast as his tiny legs would carry him, towards the lion's mighty roar.

Soon he came upon the clearing and the lion, tangled and trapped in the ropes of the hunter's net.

"Keep still, Your Majesty," cried the mouse. "I'll have you out of there in no time."

"You?" laughed the lion.

The mouse ignored him and quickly started gnawing through the net with his sharp little teeth.

Before long, there was a big hole in the net, and the lion squeezed through the ropes and escaped his trap.

The lion held out his giant paw towards the little mouse. "Thank you, my little friend," he said humbly, bowing his huge head. "I was wrong when I laughed at you and said that someone as small as you couldn't help me. You saved my life today, and I am truly grateful."

The little mouse smiled up at the lion. "You were kind enough to let me go before, and I promised I would pay you back one day," he squeaked. "It was my turn to help you."

Side by side, the big lion and little mouse walked back into the jungle. From that day on the huge, mighty lion and the tiny, mighty mouse became the best of friends.

The End

Cinderella

Once upon a time, there was a young girl who lived with her widowed father. Eventually her father remarried. His new wife had two daughters of her own. She was mean and spiteful to the young girl, and so were her daughters. They made the girl do all the housework, eat scraps and sleep by the fireplace among the cinders and ashes. Because she slept in the cinders, they called her 'Cinderella'.

One day, a letter arrived from the palace. All the women in the land were invited to attend a grand ball – where the prince would choose a bride!

Cinderella's stepsisters were very excited. Her stepmother was sure one of her daughters would marry the prince. She made Cinderella work night and day to make them as beautiful as possible. Cinderella washed and curled their dull hair. She cut and shaped their ragged nails. She stitched their ballgowns and she polished their dancing shoes until they shone.

Cinderella longed to go to the ball herself, but her stepsisters just laughed.

"You? Go to a ball?" the elder stepsister said. "But you don't have a pretty dress!"

"You? Go to a ball!" laughed the younger stepsister. "How ridiculous! You are always covered in soot and cinders!"

Tears ran down Cinderella's face as she helped her stepsisters into their dresses and jewels. At last they left for the ball. Cinderella sat alone by the fireplace. She cried and cried.

"If only I could go to the ball," she said through her tears, "and be happy for just one night. I so wish I could go."

Cinderella had barely finished speaking when there was a sparkle of light in the dull kitchen, and there stood – a fairy!

"Don't be afraid, my dear. I am your fairy godmother," the fairy said, "and you shall go to the ball!"

Cinderella stared in amazement at the fairy. Quickly, she dried her eyes.

"Really? Can I really go to the ball?" she asked, barely daring to believe it.

"If you do as I say, all will be well," the fairy answered.

"I'm used to doing as I'm told," Cinderella sniffed.

The fairy godmother told her to bring a pumpkin, four white mice and a black rat. Cinderella hurried to the garden to pick a pumpkin. She found four mice in the kitchen, and she caught a rat sleeping in the barn. With a wave of the fairy's wand, the pumpkin turned into a gleaming golden coach. Cinderella gasped in astonishment.

"It's beautiful!" she said. "But who will drive it?"

The fairy waved her wand again, and the four mice became four handsome white horses. She waved her wand a third time and the rat turned into a tall coachman.

"How wonderful!" Cinderella cried. "But I can't go to the ball in these rags."

"And you won't go in rags!" her fairy godmother cried.

She waved her wand and Cinderella's rags turned into a beautiful ballgown. Glittering glass slippers appeared on her feet. Cinderella looked lovely!

"Now, off you go," her fairy godmother said, "but remember, all this will vanish at midnight, so make sure you are home by then."

Cinderella climbed into the coach, and it whisked her away to the palace. She had never been happier.

Everyone was enchanted by the lovely stranger, especially the prince, who danced with her all evening. Cinderella enjoyed herself so much that she completely forgot her fairy godmother's warning. Suddenly, the palace clock began to strike midnight.

Bong, bong, bong...

Cinderella picked up her skirts and fled. The worried prince ran after her.

Bong, bong, bong...

She ran down the palace steps. She lost one of her glass slippers on the way, but she didn't dare stop.

Bong, bong, bong...

Cinderella jumped into the coach, and it drove off before the prince could stop her.

Bong, bong, bong!

On the final stroke of midnight, Cinderella found herself sitting on the road beside a pumpkin. Four white mice and a black rat scampered around her. She was dressed in rags and had only a single glass slipper left from her magical evening.

"Even if it was a dream," she said to herself, "it was a perfect dream."

At the palace, the prince looked longingly at the glass slipper he had found on the steps. He could not forget the wonderful girl he had danced with all night.

"I will find her," he said to himself, "and I will marry her!"

So he took the glass slipper and set out to visit every house in the land. At last he came to Cinderella's house. Her two stepsisters tried and tried to squeeze their huge feet into the delicate slipper, but no matter what they did, they could not get the slipper to fit. Cinderella watched as she scrubbed the floor.

"May I try, please?" she asked.

"You?" laughed the eldest. "You didn't even go to the ball!"

"Everyone may try," the prince said. Cinderella sat down. Her foot slipped easily into the glass slipper.

The prince took Cinderella in his arms.

"You're the one!" he said. "Will you marry me? Please?"

Cinderella's stepmother and stepsisters were furious.

"It can't be her!"

"She's just the servant!"

"She dresses in rags!"

But at that moment, the fairy godmother appeared and turned Cinderella's rags back into the fabulous ballgown. Cinderella took the other slipper from her pocket.

"Yes," Cinderella said. "Yes, it was me, and yes I will marry you."

Much to the disgust of her stepmother and stepsisters, Cinderella married the prince the very next day and went to live in the palace. The couple lived long, happy lives together, and Cinderella's stepmother and her daughters had to do their own cleaning, and never went to another ball at the palace.

The End

The Frog Prince

There was once a princess with a smile more dazzling than the sun. She lived with her father, the king, in a palace surrounded by thick woods.

When the weather was very hot, the princess would walk into the shade of the forest and sit by a pond. There she would take out her favourite toy, a golden ball that her father had given her. Over and over, she would throw it up into the air and catch it again.

One day, the ball slipped from her hand and fell into the pond with a SPLASH! The pond was so deep that she couldn't see the bottom.

"My beautiful golden ball," sobbed the princess. She cried as if her heart would break, her tears drip-dropping into the water. The princess thought her favourite toy was lost forever.

An ugly, speckled frog popped his head out of the water. "Why are you crying?" he asked.

"I have dropped my precious golden ball into the water," she cried.

"What will you give me if I fetch it back for you?" asked the frog.

"You may have my jewels and pearls. Even the crown on my head," sobbed the unhappy princess.

"I don't need any of those things," said the frog. "If you promise to care for me and be my friend, let me share food from your plate and sleep on your pillow, then I will bring back your golden ball."

"I promise," said the princess, but she didn't really mean it. As the frog swam down into the murky water, she thought, "He's only a silly old frog. I won't have to do any of those things."

When the frog swam back up with the ball, she snatched it from him and ran all the way back to the palace.

That evening, the princess was having dinner with her family when there was a knock on the door.

"Princess, let me in," called a croaky voice. When the princess went to open the door, she was horrified to find the speckled frog sitting in a puddle of water. She slammed the door and hurried back to the table.

"Why do you look so frightened?" asked the king. "Was it a witch?"

"No, father, it was a frog," replied the princess.

"What does a frog want with you?" asked the puzzled king.

The princess told her father all about losing the ball and the promise she had made to the frog.

"Princesses always keep their promises, my dear," insisted the king. "Let the frog in and make him welcome."

The princess did as she was told.

As soon as the frog hopped through the door he asked to be lifted up onto the princess's plate so that he could share her food.

When the frog saw the look of disgust on the princess's face, he sang:

"Princess, princess, fair and sweet, you made a special vow
To be my friend and share your food, so don't forget it now."

The king was annoyed to see his daughter acting so rudely. "This frog helped you when you were in trouble," he said. "You made him a promise and now you must keep it."

The princess had no choice. She lifted the damp frog onto her plate and watched as he nibbled at her food.

For the rest of the day, the frog followed the princess everywhere she went. She hoped that he would go back to his pond when it was time for bed, but he did not.

When darkness fell, the frog yawned and stretched. "I am tired," he said. "Take me to your room and let me sleep on your silken pillow."

The princess was horrified. "No, I won't!" she said. "Go back to your pond, you slimy creature, and leave me alone!"

The patient frog sang:

"Princess, princess, fair and sweet, you made a special vow
To be my friend and share your food, so don't forget it now."

The princess had no choice but to take him to her room. She couldn't bear the thought of sleeping next to him, though, so instead of placing him on her pillow, she put him in a corner on the floor. Then she climbed into her bed, laid her head down on the silken pillow and went to sleep.

After a while, the frog jumped up onto the bed. "It's draughty on the floor. Let me sleep on your pillow as you promised," he said.

The sleepy princess felt more annoyed than ever. She picked up the frog and hurled him across the room where he landed with a SMACK on the floor. The frog lay there dazed and helpless.

The princess shook herself properly awake and saw the frog lying still. She was suddenly filled with pity. She couldn't bear the thought that she might have hurt the poor thing.

"Oh, you poor darling!" she cried, and she picked him up and kissed him.

The frog transformed into a handsome young prince.

"Sweet princess," he cried. "I was bewitched and your tender kiss has broken the curse!"

The prince and princess soon fell in love and were married. They often walked in the shady forest together and sat by the pond, tossing the golden ball back and forth, and smiling at how they first met.

The End

Hansel and Gretel

Once upon a time, there were two children called Hansel and Gretel. They lived in a small cottage at the edge of the forest with their father and stepmother.

Hansel and Gretel's father was a woodcutter. He was very poor and the family didn't have much food to eat.

The day came when there was hardly any food left at all.

"What are we to do?" cried the father.

The stepmother, who didn't like Hansel and Gretel, said, "We must take the children into the thickest part of the forest and leave them there. There are just too many mouths to feed."

"We can't do that!" protested the father, for he loved his children dearly.

"We must or we'll all die of hunger!" screeched his wife. "The children are going, and that is that."

From their bedroom, Hansel and Gretel overheard the conversation. Gretel burst into tears.

"Don't worry," Hansel said. "I'll look after you."

When their parents went to bed, Hansel crept out of the house. All around lay little white pebbles that shone like coins in the silvery moonlight. He filled his pockets with them and then went back to bed.

Early the next morning, the stepmother hurried Hansel and Gretel out of bed.

“Come on, children. We’re going into the forest to chop wood,” she told them.

With a heavy heart, the woodcutter led his children into the forest. As they walked along, Hansel dropped the pebbles from his pockets onto the path.

When they reached the middle of the forest, the woodcutter said, “Wait here. We’ll be back as soon as we’ve finished chopping wood.”

Hansel and Gretel waited all day, but their father and stepmother didn’t come back. Soon, it was dark among the thick trees. Gretel was frightened.

“We’ll find our way home,” Hansel comforted his sister.

When the moon rose high in the sky, the white pebbles that Hansel had left on the path lit up. He grabbed his sister’s hand.

“Come on, Gretel, the pebbles will show us the way home!”

When Hansel and Gretel returned, the woodcutter was relieved to see his children again, but their stepmother was furious.

Before long the woodcutter and his family had very little food again.

"Tomorrow we will take the children deeper into the forest. They must not find their way home!" the stepmother cried.

This time, as they were led deep into the forest, Hansel left a trail of breadcrumbs.

When their parents didn't return from chopping wood, Hansel said, "We'll follow the breadcrumbs I dropped on the path. They will lead us home."

But when the moon came up, Hansel and Gretel couldn't see any crumbs. "The birds must have eaten them all!" whispered Hansel.

Frightened and hungry, Hansel and Gretel curled up under a tree and went to sleep, waiting anxiously for daylight.

The next morning, they wandered through the forest. After a while they came to a clearing and a little cottage.

"Hansel, look!" cried Gretel. "That cottage is made out of sweets and gingerbread!"

The children were so hungry they grabbed some sweets from the walls of the house. Just then, the door opened and an old woman hobbled out.

"Come in, children," she said, smiling. "I've got plenty more food in here."

Their stomachs growling, Hansel and Gretel followed the old woman into the cottage. After a delicious meal, she showed them to two little beds and they lay down to sleep.

The children didn't know that the old woman was actually a wicked old witch who liked to eat children!

When Hansel and Gretel woke up from their nap, the witch grabbed Hansel and locked him in a cage. She set Gretel to work cleaning and cooking huge meals to fatten up Hansel.

Weeks passed. Every morning the witch went up to the cage.

"Hold out your finger, boy. I want to feel if you are fat enough to eat."

Hansel, being a smart boy, would hold out an old chicken bone instead. The witch's eyesight was so bad that she thought the bone was Hansel's finger. She wondered why the boy wasn't getting any fatter.

One day, the witch grew impatient.

"I can't wait any longer," she screeched. "I'm going to cook Hansel now!"

Gretel was terrified.

"We'll bake some bread to eat with your brother," said the witch. "Go and check if the oven is hot enough."

Grabbing Gretel's arm, the wicked witch pushed her roughly towards the open oven door. Grinning horribly, she licked her cracked lips. She was planning on eating Gretel too, and couldn't wait for her delicious meal!

Gretel guessed the witch's trick. "I'm too big to fit in there," she said.

"Oh, you silly girl," cackled the witch. "Even I can fit in there." And she put her head into the oven to prove she was right. Gretel gave her a giant push and the witch fell right inside. Gretel quickly slammed the oven door shut.

"Hansel, the witch is dead!" cried Gretel as she unlocked her brother's cage.

As Hansel and Gretel made their way out of the house, they discovered that it was full of sparkling jewels and gold coins. The children stuffed their pockets with treasure.

"Come on, Gretel," laughed Hansel. "Let's go home!"

Their father was overjoyed to see them. He told them that their stepmother had died while they were gone and they had nothing to fear any more. Hansel and Gretel showed their father the jewels and coins. They would be poor no longer!

And from then on, the woodcutter and his children were never hungry again.

The End

The Three Billy Goats Gruff

Once upon a time, there were three goats – a little white one, a medium-sized brown one and a big grey one.

They were the Billy Goats Gruff and they were brothers.

The little Billy Goat Gruff had little horns.

The medium-sized Billy Goat Gruff had medium-sized horns.

And the big Billy Goat Gruff had big, curly horns!

The three brothers lived in a small meadow beside a river. All day long they ate the green grass.

On the other side of the river, over a rickety wooden bridge, was a huge field. The Billy Goats Gruff thought the grass there looked longer and greener and juicier!

Day after day, the three Billy Goats Gruff looked longingly at the juicy grass on the other side of the river. They would have happily crossed the bridge to go there, but for one thing.

One horrible thing.

A mean and smelly old troll with very pointy teeth lived under the bridge, and he guarded it day and night.

The grass in the meadow where the three Billy Goats Gruff lived got shorter and shorter, and drier and browner, and the brothers were getting hungrier and hungrier for fresh, juicy grass.

One day, the little Billy Goat Gruff decided he'd had enough.

"I'm so hungry!" he cried to his brothers. "I can't eat one more blade of this dry, brown grass."

"We agree!" groaned his two brothers. "Look at that juicy grass over there. Oh, if only we could get past the mean old troll."

"I'm going to try," said the little Billy Goat Gruff bravely. And off he set, TRIP TRAP, TRIP TRAP, across the bridge.

Suddenly a croaky voice roared out, "Who's that TRIP TRAPPING over my bridge? I'll eat you if you pass. You'd taste yummy in a sandwich!"

"Oh, please don't eat me," cried the little goat. He was very frightened, but he had a plan. "I'm only a little goat. My brother will be crossing in a minute, and he is much bigger and tastier than me!"

The greedy troll thought about this and burped loudly. "All right," he said, "you may cross."

The little Billy Goat Gruff ran as fast as his little legs would take him until he reached the other side.

The medium-sized goat saw his little brother munching the juicy grass on the other side of the river. He really wanted to eat that grass, too.

He turned to the big Billy Goat Gruff. "If he can cross the bridge, then so can I!" he said. And off he set, TRIP TRAP, TRIP TRAP, across the bridge.

Suddenly, the mean troll climbed out from his hiding place.

"Who's that TRIP TRAPPING over my bridge? I'll eat you if you pass. You'd taste nice with rice!" He licked his lips when he noticed how much bigger this goat was.

The medium-sized Billy Goat Gruff stopped, his hooves clacking together in fear.

"Oh, please don't eat me," he cried. "I'm really not that big. My brother will be crossing in a minute, and he is so much bigger and tastier than me!"

The troll rolled his eyes, licked dribble from his chin, and grunted that the medium-sized goat could cross the bridge.

The medium-sized Billy Goat Gruff galloped quickly across the bridge to join his little brother, before the mean troll changed his mind.

The big Billy Goat Gruff had been watching his brothers.

"I'm big and strong… and I'm really hungry!" he said to himself. So off he set, TRIP TRAP, TRIP TRAP, across the bridge to join his brothers and eat the juicy green grass on the other side.

As before, the mean, smelly troll scrabbled up onto the bridge.

"Who's that TRIP TRAPPING over my bridge? I'll eat you if you pass. You'd taste scrumptious in a stew!" This goat was big! The troll's mouth started watering and his large tummy started rumbling.

The big Billy Goat Gruff stamped his hooves. "No, you can't eat me!" he shouted. "I'm big and I have big horns, and I will toss you into the river if you don't let me pass."

Before the troll could answer, the big Billy Goat Gruff put his head down and charged at him. He tossed the mean creature high up into the air.

Down,

down,

down

fell the troll. With a huge splash, he dropped into the river and floated away. And that was the end of the mean troll.

"Maaaa! Well done, big brother!" laughed the little Billy Goat Gruff and the medium-sized Billy Goat Gruff. "Come and eat this grass – it is truly juicy and delicious!"

And the three Billy Goats Gruff were never hungry again.

The End

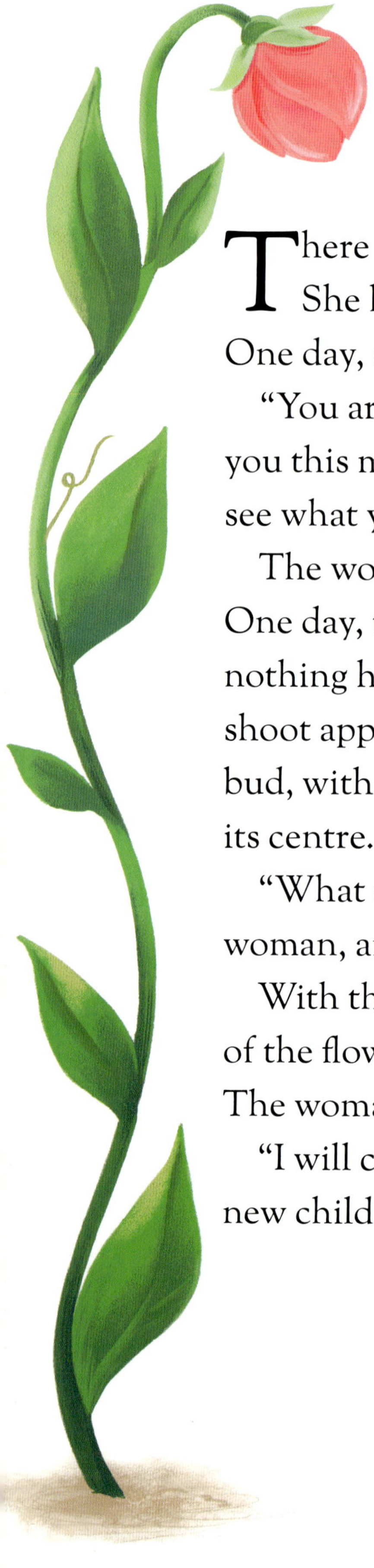

Thumbelina

There was once a poor woman who lived in a cottage. She had no husband but she longed to have a child. One day, she visited a fairy to ask for her help.

"You are a good woman," said the fairy, "so I will give you this magic seed. Plant it and water it, and you will see what you will see."

The woman thanked the fairy and did as she was told. One day, then two days, then three days passed, and nothing happened. But on the fourth day, a tiny green shoot appeared. And on the fifth day, there was a flower bud, with glossy pink petals wrapped tightly around its centre.

"What a beautiful flower you will be," smiled the woman, and she kissed it gently.

With that, the petals unfolded, and in the centre of the flower was a beautiful girl, the size of a thumb. The woman clapped her hands with joy.

"I will call you Thumbelina," she cried, and she laid her new child in a walnut-shell bed with a rose-petal quilt.

Thumbelina was very happy with her mother. Then one day, while her mother was away, an ugly, slimy toad crawled into the cottage. When she saw Thumbelina sleeping in the bed, she cried, "You'd be the perfect wife for my son!" She grabbed the girl and crept out of the cottage the same way she had come.

When Thumbelina woke up, she was sitting on a lily pad in the middle of a stream, with two warty toads staring at her.

"This is your new wife!" the mother said to her son. He opened his wide, toothless mouth in a grin, but all he could say was, "Croak! Croak!"

"I don't want to marry a toad," said Thumbelina, and she started to cry.

"You ungrateful girl!" the mother toad scolded her. "You'll stay here until you stop crying." The two toads jumped into the water and swam away. Thumbelina sobbed and sobbed.

Then, a fish took pity on her and nibbled through the lily pad's stem until it floated free. Thumbelina sailed gently downstream and escaped from the toads.

At last, she drifted to the riverbank and climbed onto dry land. Suddenly, a big brown beetle grabbed her with its claws.

"Put me down!" said Thumbelina.

"No," said the beetle. "You must stay with me and be my friend."

The beetle carried Thumbelina to a clearing. Another bigger, browner beetle was waiting for him there. He looked at Thumbelina and shook his head.

"Oh, Bertie, she's so ugly," said the bigger beetle. "She can't stay here!"

The two beetles argued and argued, waving their claws in the air, and pulling poor Thumbelina this way and that, until at last Bertie gave in and they let Thumbelina go. She ran off as fast as she could.

Thumbelina lived in the country all summer long. She missed her mother, but had no idea how to find her way home. So she busied herself collecting wild berries and making friends with the birds and small creatures she met.

Then winter came. Thumbelina was cold and hungry and all alone. Luckily, a kindly field mouse found her and invited her to stay with him in his burrow. She was so grateful that she said yes at once.

Life underground was warm and snug, but Thumbelina soon missed the sunshine. And then Mouse's friend Mole asked her to marry him.

"I don't want to marry a mole," cried Thumbelina. "And though I like living with you, Mouse, I miss the sunshine."

"You ungrateful girl!" said the mouse and the mole together. So Thumbelina sadly agreed to marry the mole and a date was set for the following summer.

Thumbelina was miserable. Then one day, as she walked through the underground tunnels, she found a swallow, almost dead with the cold. She hugged the bird against herself to warm him. He slowly opened his eyes.

"You have saved my life," said the swallow. "Come with me to the South, to the land of sunshine and flowers."

"I cannot leave Mouse," sighed Thumbelina, "he has been so kind to me."

"Then I must go alone," said the swallow, stretching his wings, "but I will return next summer. Goodbye!" Then he flew away.

Months passed and the day Thumbelina had been dreading arrived – the day she would marry the mole. As she waited for Mole to arrive, the swallow appeared again.

"Come with me now!" he cried.

"I will!" said Thumbelina.

So Thumbelina flew away to the South with the swallow. As she explored her new home, one especially beautiful flower opened in front of her. There, in the centre, was a fairy prince, no bigger than a thumb, with butterfly wings.

"Will you be my wife?" he asked at once.

"I will!" cried Thumbelina.

So Thumbelina, wearing butterfly wings made especially for her, married the prince and became Queen of the flower fairies. She did not forget her mother, and that very day arranged for fairy messengers to deliver a letter to her and a bouquet of the most beautiful flowers. And kind Thumbelina and her handsome husband lived happily ever after.

The End

The Ugly Duckling

Once upon a time, there was a proud and happy duck. "I have seven beautiful eggs and soon I will have seven beautiful ducklings," she told the other creatures of the riverbank.

It wasn't long before she heard a CRACK! And one beautiful duckling popped her little head out of the shell.

"Isn't she a beauty!" she exclaimed. Soon there was another... and then another... until she had six beautiful little ducklings, drying their fluffy yellow wings in the spring air.

"Just one egg left," quacked Mother Duck, "and it's a big one!" For quite a while, nothing happened. Mother Duck was starting to worry when, at last, the big egg began to hatch.

Tap, tap, tap! Out came a beak.

Crack, crack, crack! Out popped a head.

Crunch, crunch, crunch! Out came the last duckling.

"Oh, my!" said Mother Duck. "Isn't he... different!"

The last duckling did look strange. He was bigger than the other ducklings and didn't have such lovely yellow feathers.

"That's all right," said Mother Duck. "You're my special little duckling. Now come on into the water," she told her little ones. "You must learn to swim straight away." One by one, the ducklings hopped into the water, landing with a little plop. But the ugly duckling fell over his big feet and landed in the water with a great big SPLASH! The other ducklings laughed at their clumsy brother.

"Now, my little chicks," said Mother Duck, "stick together and stay behind me!"

Back at the nest, the ducklings practised their quacking.

"Repeat after me," said their mother. "Quack, quack, quackety-quack!"

"Quack, quack, quackety-quack!" repeated the ducklings, all except for the ugly one.

"Honk! Honk!" he called. However much he tried, he couldn't quack like his brothers and sisters.

"What a racket!" said Mother Duck. "I'm sure you'll get the hang of it soon enough."

The other ducklings all quacked with laughter.

The ugly duckling hung his head in shame.

"Nobody likes me," he thought. "I'll never fit in."

The next day, the mother duck took her little ones out for another swim. Once again, the little ducklings stayed close to her while the ugly duckling wandered alone. Some wild geese came swooping down and landed on the river nearby.

"What kind of a bird are you?" asked one goose, rather rudely.

"I'm a duckling, of course," he replied. "My family have left me all alone."

The rest of the geese felt sorry for the ugly duckling.

"Come away with us," they said. "It's a big wide world and there's so much to see!" But the ugly duckling was afraid to leave his river, so he stayed where he was.

When their mother wasn't looking, the other ducklings teased their ugly brother.

"Just look at his dull, grey feathers," said his sister unkindly, as she admired her own reflection in the water. "Mine are so much prettier!"

The ugly duckling swam away and looked at his reflection.

"I don't look the same as them," he thought.

Feeling sad and lonely, he swam down the river and didn't stop until he'd reached a place he had never seen before. "I may as well stay here by myself," he decided.

Summer turned to autumn. The sky became cloudy and the river murky. But still the ugly duckling swam alone in his quiet part of the river.

Snow fell heavily that winter and the ugly duckling was cold and lonely. The river was frozen solid.

"At least I can't see my ugly reflection any more," he thought to himself.

Spring arrived at last and the ice thawed. New visitors arrived on the river. The ugly duckling watched nervously as some magnificent white ducks swam towards him.

"You're very big ducks," he told them, when they swam close.

"We're not ducks," laughed the elegant creatures. "We're swans – just like you!"

The ugly duckling didn't know what they meant. He looked at his reflection in the river and was surprised to see beautiful white feathers and an elegant long neck.

"Is that really me?" he asked, surprised.

"Of course it is," they told him. "You are a truly handsome swan!"

The handsome young swan joined his new friends and glided gracefully back up the river with them.

When he swam past a family of ducks, Mother Duck recognized her ugly duckling straight away. "I always knew he was special," she said.

And the beautiful young swan swam down the river proudly, ruffling his magnificent white feathers and holding his elegant head high.

The End

Sleeping Beauty

Once upon a time, there lived a king and queen. When the queen gave birth to a beautiful baby girl, the king and queen were filled with joy and decided to hold a christening feast to celebrate. They invited their friends, and all the kings, queens, princes and princesses from other kingdoms all over the land.

Five good fairies lived in the kingdom, and the king wanted them to be godmothers to his daughter. One of these fairies was very old, and no one had seen her in years or even knew where she was. So when the king sent out the invitations to his daughter's christening, he invited only the four young fairies.

The day of the christening arrived. It was a joyous occasion and the palace was full of laughter and dancing.

After the delicious feast, the four good fairies gave the princess their magical gifts.

Bending over the crib, the first fairy waved her wand and said, "You shall be kind and considerate."

The second fairy said, "You shall be beautiful and loving."

The third fairy said, "You shall be clever and thoughtful."

The baby girl was promised everything in the world that you could wish for. But just as the third fairy finished giving her gift, there was a loud bang, and the palace doors flew open.

It was the old fairy. She was furious because she hadn't been invited to the feast. She rushed over to the sleeping baby and waved her wand, casting a curse upon the child.

"One day the king's daughter shall prick her finger on a spindle and fall down dead!" she screeched.

And then she left.

The guests fell silent at these terrible words and the queen burst into tears.

The fourth fairy had not yet given her gift. "Dear Queen, please do not weep. I cannot undo the curse, but I can soften it," she said.

She walked to the crib and waved her wand.

"The princess will prick her finger on a spindle, but she will not die. Instead, the princess and everyone within the palace and its grounds will fall into a deep sleep that will last for one hundred years."

The king thanked the fairy for her kindness and then, to protect his daughter, ordered that every spindle in the kingdom be burnt.

The years passed and the princess grew into a beautiful and kind young woman, just as the fairies had promised.

One day, to amuse herself, the princess decided to explore the rooms in the palace that she had never been in before.

After a while, she came to a little door at the top of a tall tower. Inside, there was an old woman working at her spinning wheel. The princess didn't know that the woman was really the old fairy in disguise.

"What are you doing?" the princess asked curiously.

"I'm spinning thread, dear child," replied the woman.

"Can I try?" said the princess.

No sooner had she touched the spindle than she pricked her finger and fell into a deep, deep sleep.

A strange quietness came over the palace, from the gardens to the tallest tower, and the king and queen began to yawn.

Before long, every living thing within the castle walls had fallen into a deep, deep sleep.

As time passed, a hedge of thorns sprang up around the palace. It grew higher and thicker every year, until only the tallest towers could be seen above it.

The story of the beautiful princess that lay sleeping within its walls spread throughout the land. She became known as Sleeping Beauty.

Many princes tried to break through the thorns to rescue Sleeping Beauty, but none were successful. The thorn hedge was too thick.

Exactly one hundred years after the princess had fallen asleep, a handsome prince, having heard the story of Sleeping Beauty, decided to try and break the curse and awaken the sleeping princess.

The prince didn't know that the fairy's spell was coming to its end. As he pushed against the thick hedge, every thorn turned into a beautiful rose, and a path magically formed to let him pass.

Soon the prince came to the palace. Not a sound could be heard anywhere. He saw people and animals asleep in every room.

At last he found the tiny room in the tower where Sleeping Beauty lay. The prince looked at her in wonder and then kissed her gently.

The sleeping princess opened her eyes and smiled up at the prince. With that one look, they fell in love.

All around the palace, other people were waking up. The king and queen stirred from their deep sleep and were overjoyed to see their daughter awake. They welcomed the handsome prince who had found their princess.

The palace was once again filled with laughter and joy.

The king called for a huge wedding feast to be prepared, and he invited everyone in the entire kingdom.

Sleeping Beauty married her handsome prince and they lived happily ever after.

The End

How the Leopard Got His Spots

Long, long ago, Leopard lived on a hot, bare, sandy-yellow plain in Africa. Giraffe and Zebra lived there too, along with lots of deer, big and small, young and old. The animals were sandy-yellow all over, just like the plain itself. Leopard was sandy-yellow, too, which wasn't good for the rest of the animals because Leopard was hard to spot on the sandy-yellow plain. He could lie in wait in the sandy-yellow grasses, then jump out, catch them and eat them up whenever he wanted to. Giraffe and Zebra and the rest of the animals lived in fear. Leopard, however, was very happy and never hungry!

After a while, Giraffe and Zebra and the others had had enough. They decided to move away from the sandy plain to find a better place to live. They walked and walked until they came to a huge forest where the sun shone through the trees making stripy, speckly, patchy shadows, and sections of spotty, stripy sunshine. The animals hid themselves there, and while they hid, partly in the sun, partly in the shadows, their skins changed colour. Giraffe's skin became covered with big, brown, blotchy spots from the blotchy shadow he stood in, and Zebra's skin became covered with stripes from the stripy shadow he lay in. The other animals' skin became darker, too, with wavy lines and patterns from the shadows around them.

Back on the sandy plain, Leopard was puzzled. All the animals had disappeared and he was starting to get hungry.

"Where have they all gone?" he asked Baboon.

"To the forest," said Baboon carelessly. "And they've changed. You need to change too."

Leopard started to ask Baboon what she meant by 'change', but Baby Baboon needed feeding, so she was too busy to explain.

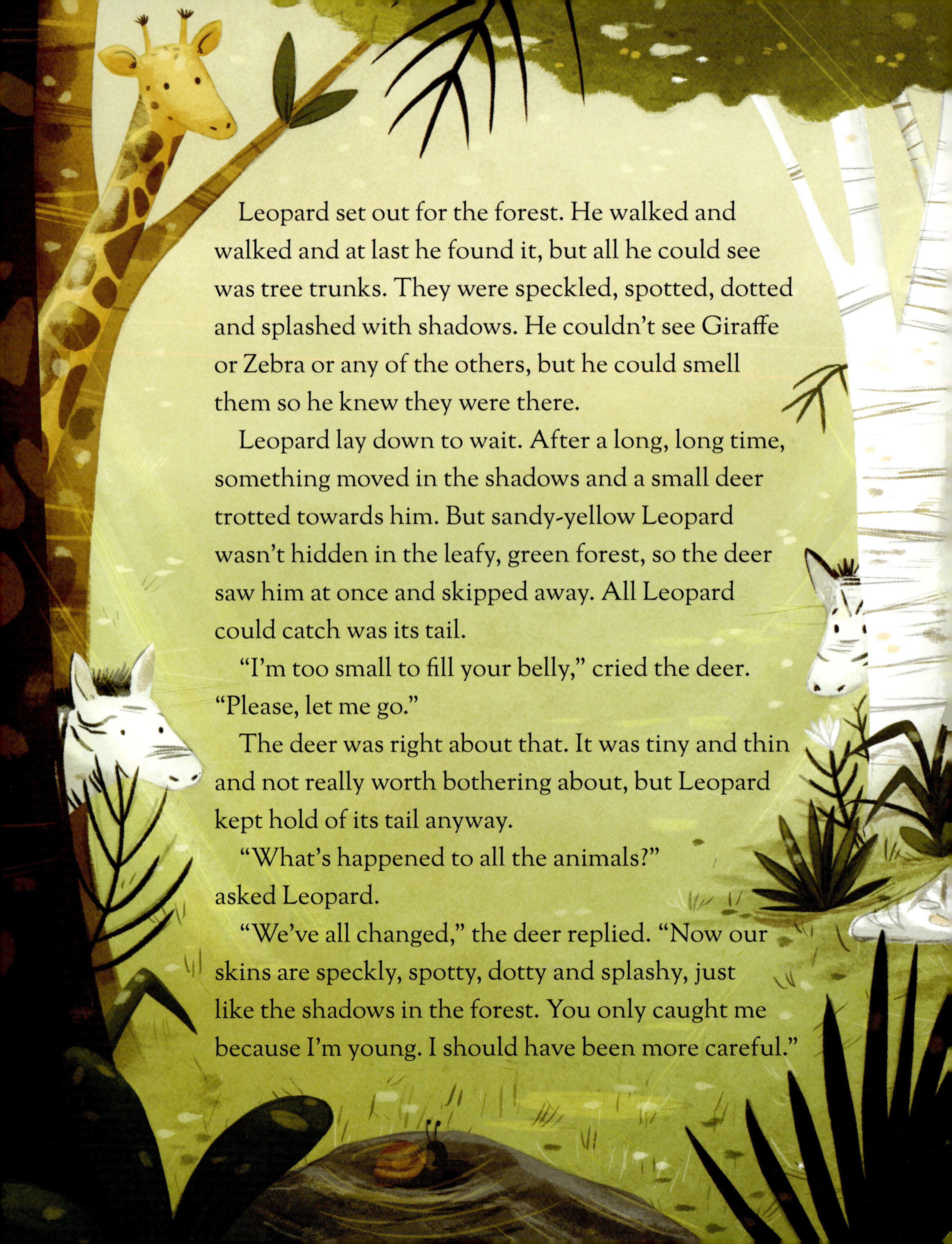

Leopard set out for the forest. He walked and walked and at last he found it, but all he could see was tree trunks. They were speckled, spotted, dotted and splashed with shadows. He couldn't see Giraffe or Zebra or any of the others, but he could smell them so he knew they were there.

Leopard lay down to wait. After a long, long time, something moved in the shadows and a small deer trotted towards him. But sandy-yellow Leopard wasn't hidden in the leafy, green forest, so the deer saw him at once and skipped away. All Leopard could catch was its tail.

"I'm too small to fill your belly," cried the deer. "Please, let me go."

The deer was right about that. It was tiny and thin and not really worth bothering about, but Leopard kept hold of its tail anyway.

"What's happened to all the animals?" asked Leopard.

"We've all changed," the deer replied. "Now our skins are speckly, spotty, dotty and splashy, just like the shadows in the forest. You only caught me because I'm young. I should have been more careful."

Leopard let the little deer go and sat down to think. "So that's why I can't see Giraffe and Zebra and the rest of them in the forest," he thought. "They've changed their skins to match the shadowy trees. If I'm going to catch them, do I need to change too? And how in the world can I do that?"

As he sat there thinking, more deer walked through the trees. When they moved, Leopard could see them clearly. When they stopped moving, they were hidden by the shadows. Leopard was easy to spot with his sandy-yellow skin, so the deer didn't come too close.

Leopard sat in the shadows a long, long time and licked his paws thoughtfully. Soon he began to notice something odd. His paws weren't sandy-yellow any more. They had small, dark spots on them. And there were spots on his tail, too.

Leopard looked around and realised that the spots on his skin matched the small, dark patches of shadow he was lying in. "Ah-ha!" he thought. "The shadows have made these spots, just in the time that I've been lying here. That's how I can change my skin, just like Giraffe and Zebra and the rest of them!"

By this time, Leopard had grown tired from all the thinking and waiting, so he lay down and fell into a deep sleep. When he awoke a long, long time later, his skin was completely covered in small, dark spots, made by the shadows of the forest.

"Well, how wonderful!" he said, looking at his new skin. "Now my skin is no longer sandy-yellow-brownish, I can hide in the leafy, green forest so that Giraffe and Zebra and the rest of them can't see me. Then, when they come close, I can leap out to catch them and eat them up!"

With that, the spotty Leopard set off into the speckly, blotchy, stripy shade of the deep forest where he lived happily ever after, eating and sleeping and not being spotted. And the other animals learned to hide from him as best as they could, too!

The End

The Gingerbread Man

Once upon a time, a little old woman and a little old man lived by themselves in a little old cottage. One day the little old woman decided to bake a treat for the little old man.

"I'll make him a special gingerbread man," she thought.

She mixed all the ingredients together, rolled out the dough, cut out the gingerbread man and popped him in the oven to bake.

Soon a delicious smell filled the little old cottage.

The little old woman was just putting on her oven gloves to check her baking, when she heard a strange voice calling out.

"Let me out! I've finished baking and it's hot in here!"

The little old woman looked around. She was confused. "I must be hearing voices!" she chuckled to herself.

She opened the oven door and nearly fell over in surprise when the little gingerbread man jumped up off the baking tray, rushed past her and ran out through the front door.

"Come back," cried the little old woman. "You smell delicious. We want to eat you!"

But the gingerbread man was too fast for the little old woman. He ran into the garden and past the little old man.

"Stop!" cried the little old man, setting down his wheelbarrow. "I want to eat you!"

But the little gingerbread man was already halfway down the road outside the little old cottage. He was very fast, and the little old woman and the little old man were very slow.

"Stop! Stop!" they wheezed, out of breath, as they ran down the road.

The gingerbread man darted under a fence into a field, singing as he went:

"Run, run, as fast as you can,
You can't catch me, I'm the
gingerbread man!"

As the gingerbread man ran through the field, he passed a pig.

"Stop!" snorted the pig. "I want to eat you!"

"I've run away from a little old woman and a little old man, and I can run away from you," he said.

And he ran even faster, followed by the little old woman, the little old man and the pig.

Soon the little gingerbread man met a cow.

"You smell scrumptious!" mooed the cow. "Stop, little man, I want to eat you!"

But the gingerbread man just ran faster. "I've run away from a little old woman, a little old man and a pig, and I can run away from you," he cried.

The cow started to run after the gingerbread man, but he sprinted past her through the tall grass in the field, singing out:

"Run, run, as fast as you can,
You can't catch me, I'm the gingerbread man!"

The little old woman, the little old man, the pig and the cow ran and ran, but none of them could catch the little gingerbread man.

In the next field, the gingerbread man met a horse.

"You look yummy!" neighed the horse. "Stop, little man, I want to eat you!"

But the gingerbread man just ran faster. "I have run away from a little old woman, a little old man, a pig and a cow, and I can run away from you!" he cried.

The horse started to gallop after the gingerbread man, but he was already halfway across the field. He turned and waved at the horse as he sang out:

"Run, run, as fast as you can,
You can't catch me, I'm the gingerbread man!"

The little old woman, the little old man, the pig, the cow and the horse ran and ran, but none of them could catch the little gingerbread man.

The little gingerbread man squeezed through a hedge and ran on, faster and faster, along a path through a shady wood. He grinned, feeling very pleased with himself, and rather proud of how fast he could run.

"No one can catch me!" he giggled.

But just a little further on down the woodland path, the gingerbread man came to an abrupt stop. There before him flowed a wide river, completely blocking his way.

While the little gingerbread man was wondering how he was going to get across the river, a sly old fox came up to him.

"Hello, little man," said the fox, licking his lips. "You look like you could do with some help."

"Oh, yes please," cried the gingerbread man. "I've run away from a little old woman, a little old man, a pig, a cow and a horse, and I need to get across this river so that I can keep on running. And I can't swim!"

"Well, jump on my back, and I'll carry you across the river," grinned the sly old fox. "You'll be safe and dry."

So the little gingerbread man climbed onto the fox's tail and the fox began to swim across the river.

After a while, the fox said, "You're too heavy for my tail. Jump onto my back."

The little gingerbread man ran lightly down the fox's tail and jumped onto his back, clinging tightly onto his fur.

Soon, the fox said, "You're too heavy for my back. Jump onto my nose."

The little gingerbread man did as he was told and jumped onto the fox's nose.

At last, they reached the other side of the river. The gingerbread man was just about to jump to the ground when the hungry fox threw back his head. The little gingerbread man suddenly found himself tossed high in the air.

Then down fell the gingerbread man and SNAP! went the mouth of the sly old fox.

And that was the end of the little gingerbread man!

The End

The Town Mouse and the Country Mouse

Once upon a time, there were two little mice. One of them lived in the town, and the other one lived in the country.

One day, the Town Mouse went to visit the Country Mouse. He had never been to the country before so he was very excited. He packed a small suitcase and went on his way.

Country Mouse's home was small and dark – not at all like Town Mouse's home. Lunch was very different too. There was creamy cheese, juicy apples and crispy, crunchy hazelnuts. It was all very tasty, but when Town Mouse had finished, he was still hungry.

After lunch, Country Mouse took Town Mouse for a walk. They went down a sunny path, through a creaky gate and into a large field. Town Mouse was just starting to enjoy himself when...

"Moo!"

"What was that?" he asked nervously, scurrying closer to Country Mouse.

"Ha! That's just a cow," said his friend. "There are lots of them in the country. It's nothing to be scared of."

Town Mouse and Country Mouse strolled on, through a flowery meadow and over a grassy hill. Soon, they came to a peaceful pond. Town Mouse was just starting to enjoy himself when...

"Hiss!"

"What was that?" he asked again, quivering from nose to tail.

"Ha! That's just a goose," said his friend. "There are lots of them in the country. It's nothing to be scared of."

Town Mouse and Country Mouse carried on walking, across a rickety bridge, down a sandy track, and into a shady wood. Town Mouse was just starting to enjoy himself when...

"Twit-twoo!"

"What was that?" he yelped, and he jumped off the ground in terror.

"It's an owl!" cried Country Mouse. "Run for your life! If it catches you, it will eat you up!"

So the two mice ran and ran until they found a leafy hedge to hide in.

Town Mouse was terrified. "I don't like the country at all!" he said. "Come to stay with me in the town. You'll see how much better it is!"

Country Mouse had never been to the town before, so he packed a small rucksack and went to stay with his friend.

Town Mouse's home was huge and grand, not at all like Country Mouse's home.

Lunch was very different too! Instead of apples and nuts, there were sandwiches and cupcakes and chocolates. Lots and lots of them. It was tasty, but soon Country Mouse began to feel a bit ill.

After dinner, the friends went out for a walk. They walked past shops and offices and houses. Country Mouse was just starting to enjoy himself when...

"Beep-beep!"

"What's that?" he asked fearfully, looking about him.

"That? It's just a car," said his friend. "There are lots of them in the town. It's nothing to be afraid of."

Then the mice walked through a park, past a church and down a wide road. Country Mouse was just starting to enjoy himself when...

"Nee-nah! Nee-nah!"

"What's that?" he asked again, his whiskers twitching.

"That? It's just a fire engine. There are lots of them in the town. It's nothing to be afraid of."

As the mice pitter-pattered home they passed a playground, a school and a pretty garden. Country Mouse was just starting to enjoy himself when...

"Meow!"

"What's that?" he squeaked, his eyes as wide as saucers.

"It's a cat!" cried Town Mouse. "Run for your life! If it catches you, it will eat you up!"

So the two mice ran and ran, all the way back to Town Mouse's home.

Country Mouse was terrified! "I don't like the town at all! I'm going home," he said.

"But how can you be happy living near the cow and the goose and that horrible owl?" said Town Mouse.

"They don't scare me!" cried Country Mouse. "How can you be happy living near the cars and the fire engines and that terrible cat?"

"They don't scare me!" cried Town Mouse.

The two mice looked at each other. Who was right and who was wrong? They would simply never agree. So they shook hands and went their separate ways: Town Mouse to his grand home and Country Mouse to his cosy one.

"Home, sweet home!" said the Town Mouse, sighing a deep, happy sigh.

"Home, sweet home!" said the Country Mouse, smiling a big, happy smile.

And the two of them lived happily ever after, each in their own way.

The End

Rumpelstiltskin

Once upon a time, there was a poor miller who had just one daughter. She was very beautiful and he told many people about her.

One day, the king rode through the village. The miller desperately wanted to impress the king. "Your Highness, my daughter is very pretty and smart," he said.

But the king took no notice.

"She can also spin straw into gold!" the miller lied.

"Your daughter must be very clever. Bring her to the palace tomorrow so I can see for myself," demanded the king.

The miller didn't dare disobey the king, so the next day he brought his daughter to the palace. The king led the girl to a room filled with straw. On the floor stood a little stool and a spinning wheel.

"Spin this straw into gold by tomorrow morning, or you will be thrown into the dungeon," said the king. Then he left the room and locked the door.

The poor miller's daughter sat down on the stool and gazed at all the straw around her. She wept bitterly at the impossible task before her.

All of a sudden, the door sprang open and in came the strangest little man she had ever seen.

"Why are you crying?" he asked.

"I have to spin all this straw into gold before the morning, but I don't know how," replied the girl sadly.

"If you give me your pretty necklace, I will spin the straw into gold," said the strange little man.

"Oh, thank you!" gasped the girl, wiping away her tears and handing over her necklace.

The little man sat down in front of the spinning wheel and set to work.

All night long, the little man spun, and by morning the room was filled with reels of gold. And just as suddenly as he had appeared, the strange man disappeared.

When the king arrived, he was astonished to see so much gold.

"You have done very well," he said, "but I wonder if you can do the same thing again?"

He took the miller's daughter to a much bigger room. It, too, was filled with straw.

"Spin this straw into gold by tomorrow morning, or you will be thrown into the dungeon," said the king, and once more he locked the girl in the room.

The miller's daughter was very frightened. The strange little man appeared before her again.

"Don't cry," he said. "Give me your shiny ring, and I will spin the straw into gold."

She handed over her ring gratefully, and the little man set to work. Once again, all the straw was turned into gold.

The king wanted to try one more time.

"If you can do this again, you shall be my queen!" cried the king.

The poor miller's daughter wept even more bitterly this time when the king left.

"Why are you crying?" said the little man, appearing for the third time. "You know that I will help you."

"But I have nothing left to give you," sobbed the girl.

"If you become queen," replied the little man, "you can give me your first-born child."

The desperate miller's daughter agreed to the man's request. And once again, he spun all the straw into gold.

The king was so delighted when he saw all the gold the next day that he kept his promise and married the miller's daughter.

The new queen was very happy and soon forgot about the promise she had made to the strange little man who saved her from the dungeon.

A year later, the king and queen had a beautiful baby boy.

Late one night, the little man appeared in the queen's bedroom as she watched over her sleeping baby.

"I'm here for your baby," he said. "Just as you promised."

The queen was horrified. "Oh, please, take all my jewels and money instead," she begged. "Not my son!"

"No," replied the little man. "You made a promise. But I will give you three days. If in that time you can guess my name, then you will keep your baby."

The desperate queen agreed. The next day she sent messengers all over the kingdom to collect all the boys' names they could find.

That night, the strange man appeared again, and the queen read out the names she had gathered. But after each name he just laughed.

The next day, the queen sent her messengers out to find even more names, and that night she read out the new names when the little man appeared. But once again, the queen's guesses were wrong.

On the third day, the poor queen was in despair. It was getting late by the time her last messenger returned.

"Your Highness, I haven't found any new names," he said, "but as I was returning through the forest, I saw a little man leaping and dancing around a fire, singing a song. It went like this:

'The queen will never win my game,
For Rumpelstiltskin is my name!'"

The queen was overjoyed!

When the little man appeared that night, the queen said, "Are you perhaps called... Rumpelstiltskin?"

The little man was furious. He stamped his foot so hard it went through the floor. Then, pulling on his leg until he was free, he stomped out of the room and was never seen or heard from again.

And the king and queen, and their son, lived happily ever after.

The End

The Golden Goose

There was once a man who lived at the edge of a forest. He had three sons. One day, the eldest boy went to cut wood. His mother gave him a cake and some fresh milk to take. After a short time, a little old man with a grey beard approached him.

"Would you please give me something to eat and drink?" the man asked. "I am very hungry and thirsty." But the boy refused.

"I won't have enough for myself if I share it with you," he said, and he carried on cutting wood. A short while later, the axe slipped and cut the boy's arm. He went home to have it bandaged.

The second son said that he would go to cut wood instead. His mother gave him a cake and some fresh milk. Once again, the old man approached and asked for a share.

"No," the boy said, "because whatever I give to you I can't have myself."

Soon after, his axe also slipped and cut his leg. He limped home to have his leg bandaged.

The youngest boy, Billy, then said that he would go to cut wood. His father refused.

"You are a silly boy. Your brothers have hurt themselves, so you certainly will too," he said.

But Billy insisted. At last, his mother gave him a dry biscuit and a bottle of plain water and he set off into the forest. No sooner had he started work than the old man appeared and asked for a drink and a bite to eat.

"It's plain food," Billy said, "but if you're happy with dry biscuit and water, I'll gladly share with you."

They shared the biscuit and water, then the little old man said, "You have been good to me, and you will have your reward. Cut down that tree over there and see what you find inside it."

Billy did as the man said. Hidden inside the tree trunk he found a goose with shining feathers of pure gold! Billy wondered how there could be such a strange bird. He looked around for the old man, but he had vanished, so Billy picked up the goose and set off for home.

Before long, Billy was totally lost. It was growing dark, so when he came to an inn he decided to stay the night.

The innkeeper had three daughters. They were very curious about the golden goose. When Billy went for supper, the eldest girl thought she would steal a single feather. As soon as she put her hand on the goose, she stuck fast to it! No matter how she struggled, she couldn't get free.

The middle girl, also wanting a feather, tried to push her sister out of the way, but found that she became stuck fast to her sister's arm.

When the youngest girl approached, her sisters warned her not to touch them. But she thought they were trying to keep the golden feathers all for themselves. She took hold of the middle sister's arm, and immediately she stuck like glue.

The next morning, Billy set off down the street with the golden goose, dragging the girls behind him. As they passed a church, the parson called out, "What are you girls doing, running after that young man? Let go at once!"

He tried to pull the youngest girl away, but he was then as stuck as they were. The parson called to his wife to free him, but that just ended with the wife sticking to the parson.

Two farmers ran from their fields to help the strange group, and soon they were stuck fast, too.

By now there were seven people in a line following behind the boy with his golden goose. It was the strangest procession you could imagine!

It happened that they passed near the king's palace. He had a daughter, but she was always miserable. No one could make the princess smile, let alone laugh. The king was so desperate to cheer her up that he had promised her hand in marriage to anyone who could make her happy. Many young men had tried to amuse her, telling jokes, doing tricks, fooling around and pulling faces, but nothing worked – she was as sad as ever.

When the princess looked out of her window that day and saw Billy walking along the street carrying a golden goose, she started to smile.

Then she saw the three sisters, the parson, the parson's wife and the two farmers staggering along behind. Her smile turned to a laugh and her laugh became louder and louder. She laughed so hard that tears ran down her cheeks.

"My dear, what has made you laugh?" the king cried, delighted. The princess was laughing so much she couldn't speak. She could only point at Billy and the long line of people stuck to the goose.

The king sent a footman to bring Billy to the palace.

"The princess is laughing!" the king exclaimed. "You made her laugh! That means you may marry her!"

"I? Marry the princess?" Billy said.

"Why, yes," the king answered. "I am so glad that at last someone has helped my poor, sad daughter. All I want is for her to be happy – if you can make her smile and laugh, you are the best husband she could have."

Suddenly the golden goose jumped from Billy's arms, and all the people toppled backwards, unstuck.

Billy and the princess soon married, and they lived long, happy lives full of smiles and laughter.

The End

The Elves and the Shoemaker

There was once a shoemaker who lived with his wife. Although they worked from dawn until dusk, they were very poor.

"We have only enough leather to make one more pair of shoes to sell," the shoemaker told his wife one day.

"What will become of us?" asked the shoemaker's wife. "How can we live without money?"

The shoemaker shook his head sadly. He cut out the leather and left it on his workbench, ready to start work the next morning.

Then the couple went to bed with heavy hearts.

In the middle of the night, when the house was quiet and pale moonlight shone into the workshop, two elves appeared. They were dressed in rags but had eyes as bright as buttons. They explored the workshop, balancing on cotton reels and peering into cupboards. Soon they found the leather.

Elves are busy little creatures and so they set to work at once, snipping and sewing. As they worked, they sang:

"Busy little elves are we,
Working by the pale moonlight.
While the humans are asleep,
We are busy through the night!"

By dawn, the two little elves had finished their work and disappeared.

When the shoemaker came to start work the next morning, he could not believe his eyes. There, on his workbench, was the finest pair of shoes he had ever seen.

"The stitches are so delicate," he said, as he showed his astonished wife the beautiful shoes. "I will place them in my window for everyone to see."

Soon, a rich gentleman walked by the shop. He saw the stylish shoes and came inside.

The rich gentleman tried on the shoes and they fitted perfectly. He was so delighted that he gave the shoemaker twice the asking price.

"I can buy more leather!" said the shoemaker happily to his wife.

That evening, the shoemaker cut out the leather for two more pairs of shoes. He left it on his workbench for the next morning.

In the middle of the night, the two elves appeared again. They explored the workshop, climbing on the tools and swinging from shoelaces. Soon they found the leather.

The elves set to work at once, snipping and sewing. As they worked, they sang:

"Busy little elves are we,
Working by the pale moonlight.
While the humans are asleep,
We are busy through the night!"

By dawn, the two little elves had finished their work and disappeared.

Once again the shoemaker came into his workshop and found the shoes, neatly finished on his bench. The shoemaker placed them in his window.

By now, the rich gentleman had told his friends about the shoemaker's fine work. The two pairs of shoes sold that same day for more money than the shoemaker could ever have dreamed of. The shoemaker now had enough money to buy leather to make four new pairs of shoes.

"But who can be helping us?" asked the shoemaker's wife.

That evening, the shoemaker cut out the leather for four more pairs of shoes. He left it on his workbench as usual. Then, the shoemaker and his wife hid and waited.

In the middle of the night, they watched in amazement as the two little elves appeared. As usual, the elves explored the workshop. They danced with colourful ribbons and juggled pretty beads. Soon they found the leather. Again, the elves set to work, snipping and sewing. As they worked, they sang:

"Busy little elves are we,
Working by the pale moonlight.
While the humans are asleep,
We are busy through the night!"

By dawn, the two little elves had finished their work and disappeared.

"We must repay our little helpers for their kindness," said the shoemaker to his wife.

The couple thought hard about what they could do to thank the elves.

"They were dressed in rags," said the shoemaker's wife. "Why don't we make them some fine new clothes?"

Although they were now very busy in their shop, the shoemaker and his wife spent every spare moment they had making their gift for the elves. They cut out fine cloth and leather, and sewed tiny seams. Soon they had made two little pairs of trousers, two smart coats, two sturdy pairs of boots and two warm, woolly scarves. They placed the little outfits on the workbench for the elves to find.

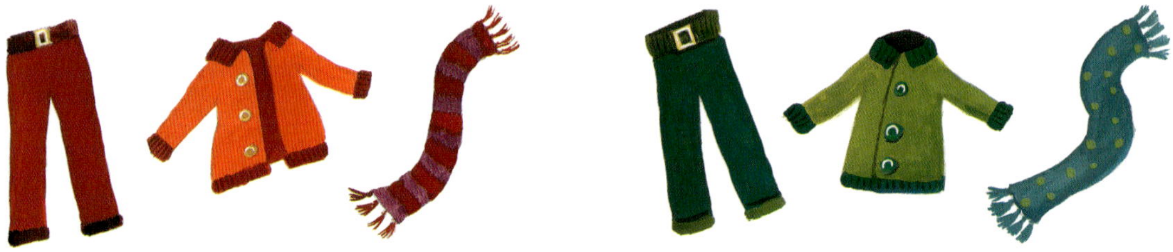

That night, when the house was quiet and pale moonlight shone into the workshop, the shoemaker and his wife hid and waited. They watched happily as the two little elves appeared. As usual, the elves explored the workshop. They made a tightrope from thread and bounced on a pincushion. Soon they found the tiny little outfits. They were delighted! They put on the trousers, the coats, the boots and the scarves and danced merrily around the workbench.

As they danced, they sang:

"Handsome little elves are we,
Dancing by the pale moonlight.
While the humans are asleep,
We make merry through the night!"

And then, the smart little elves put on their hats and disappeared.

The shoemaker and his wife never saw the little elves again. But the couple continued to make fine shoes for their shop and from that day on they always prospered.

The End

The Tortoise and the Hare

The hare and the tortoise were neighbours. Hare was always in a hurry, rushing from one important task to another. He was so fast and busy that sometimes he could barely remember where he was going. Tortoise, on the other hand, plodded steadily along. He didn't go to many different places in a day, but he always got where he needed to be.

One day, Tortoise was walking slowly along the road when Hare sped past him. Hare looked over his shoulder and called out, "Hurry up, Tortoise – you'll never get there!"

"I will," Tortoise said calmly, "I will. Slow, but steady."

Hare turned back and ran around Tortoise three times, laughing. Then he ran on.

Half an hour later, Hare came back. Tortoise was still going in the same direction, and he hadn't got very far. Hare laughed.

"You're so slow!" he said. "How do you ever get anywhere?"

"Look," Tortoise said. "One step at a time. One foot after the other. Slow, but steady."

"You're hopeless!" Hare said. "It will take you all day just to get to the end of the road!"

At last, Tortoise was too cross to ignore Hare any longer.

"I get everywhere I want to go!" he said. "And if you don't believe me, I'll challenge you to a race. You can pick the route, the day and the time."

Hare laughed until he fell over. He rolled around on the floor, tears running along his whiskers.

"A race?" he gasped. "Between you and me? That's ridiculous! You don't stand a chance."

"Are you scared?" Tortoise asked. "Because if not, let's do it."

Hare could hardly stop laughing, but they arranged the race for the next day and asked Fox to judge it. They would start from an old oak tree and race all the way to the river.

Tortoise set out early that evening so that he would be at the start line on time in the morning.

Hare went home for a long sleep and got up late. He ran to the oak tree and found Tortoise ready and waiting. All the other animals had come out to watch.

"Fox is waiting for you at the river," Bear said. "We can start whenever you're ready."

Hare and Tortoise got into position.

"On your marks," said Tortoise.

"Get set," said Hare.

"Go!" shouted all the animals.

And off went the tortoise and the hare.

Hare sprinted ahead, bounding along the path. Tortoise lifted one foot, and put it down. Then he lifted the other foot, and put it down. Slowly, slowly. By the time Tortoise reached the first bush, Hare was a tiny spot in the distance. By the time he reached the second bush, Hare was nowhere to be seen.

After a few minutes, Hare could see the river ahead. He paused and looked around. He couldn't see Tortoise at all.

"He is so slow!" he laughed to himself. "He won't be here for hours. I might as well have a rest." So Hare sat down under a tree not far from the finish line. The sun was warm, and the lazy buzz of bees visiting the flowers around him was soothing. Soon Hare dozed off.

Back along the path, Tortoise carried on, slow but steady, one step at a time, one foot after the other.

After an hour, Hare woke up and peered into the distance. He could just see Tortoise coming towards him, slow but steady, and still far away.

"He's so slow!" Hare said to himself. "He won't be here for hours. I might as well go back to sleep." And that's just what he did.

Tortoise carried on, slow but steady, his heavy shell wobbling along the path. Hare slept on in the hot sun.

When Hare woke up, he couldn't see Tortoise anywhere.

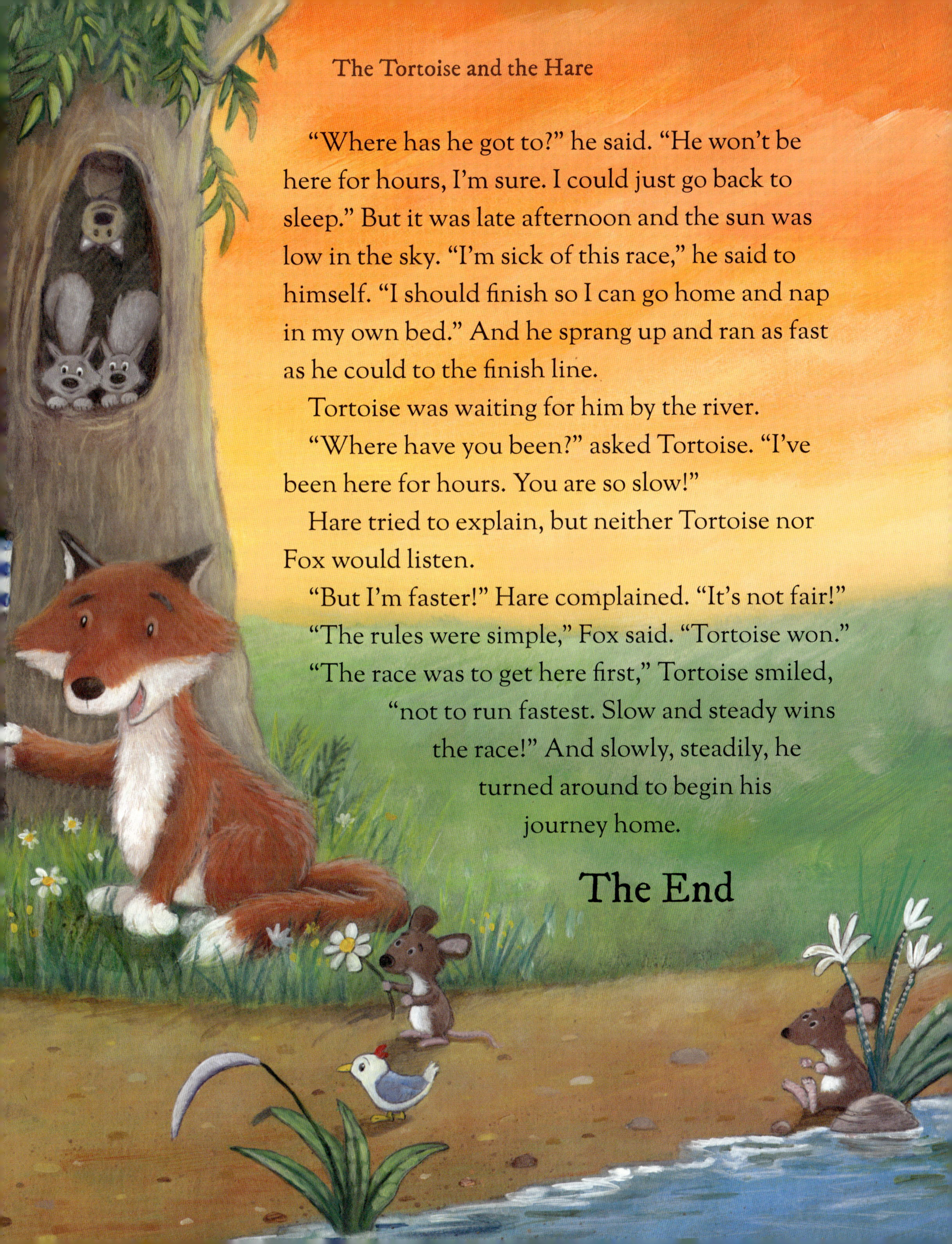

"Where has he got to?" he said. "He won't be here for hours, I'm sure. I could just go back to sleep." But it was late afternoon and the sun was low in the sky. "I'm sick of this race," he said to himself. "I should finish so I can go home and nap in my own bed." And he sprang up and ran as fast as he could to the finish line.

Tortoise was waiting for him by the river.

"Where have you been?" asked Tortoise. "I've been here for hours. You are so slow!"

Hare tried to explain, but neither Tortoise nor Fox would listen.

"But I'm faster!" Hare complained. "It's not fair!"

"The rules were simple," Fox said. "Tortoise won."

"The race was to get here first," Tortoise smiled, "not to run fastest. Slow and steady wins the race!" And slowly, steadily, he turned around to begin his journey home.

The End

The Princess and the Pea

Once upon a time, in a kingdom far away, there lived a handsome prince. He had loving parents, plenty of friends and lived a wonderful life in his castle. But one thing made him sad. He did not have a wife.

The prince had always wanted to marry a princess. But he wanted her to be clever and funny, and loving and kind. None of the princesses that he met at parties and balls were quite right.

Some of the princesses were too mean, some were too rude.

Some were too quiet, some were too loud.

And some were just plain boring!

So, the prince decided to travel the world in the hope of finding a perfect princess. He met many more princesses who tried to impress him with their beauty, their dancing and their baking... but still none were quite right.

"I'm never going to meet the right princess," he sighed to himself. "Oh, where is that girl of my dreams?"

Months passed without success, so eventually the prince headed back to his castle.

"Cheer up, my son," said the king. "You are still young. One day you will meet a wonderful girl, just like I met your mother." The king smiled at the queen, but he was at a loss to know how to make the prince happy again.

Then one night, when even the king and queen had begun to give up hope of their son ever finding a bride, there was a terrible storm. Thunder roared, lightning flashed and the rain poured down.

Suddenly there was a loud knock on the wooden castle door.

"I wonder who could be out on such a terrible stormy night?" said the prince. When he opened the door, a pretty young girl stared back at him. She was soaked from head to toe.

"Oh please, Your Royal Highness, may I come in for a moment?" she pleaded. "I was travelling to see some friends, but I got lost in this storm, and now I am very cold and very wet."

The prince ushered the poor girl in out of the wind and the rain.

"You poor thing," said the queen. "You must stay the night. You cannot travel on in this weather."

The prince smiled at the girl. "What is your name?" he asked her.

"I'm Princess Penelope," she replied. "You are all very kind. I don't want to be a bother to you."

At the word princess, the queen smiled to herself. "I wonder..." she thought, but she didn't say anything. She took the girl's hand and said aloud, "Of course not, my dear. Come, and let's get you warm."

Once the princess had changed into some dry clothes, the queen invited her to have some supper with the family.

The prince listened contentedly as the charming princess chatted away over their meal. He could not stop gazing at her. She was clever and funny, and loving and kind. By the end of the evening the prince had fallen in love!

The queen was delighted when she saw what was happening, but she wanted to be quite sure that Princess Penelope was a real princess. She went to the guest room in the castle and placed a tiny pea under the mattress. Then she told the servants to pile twenty more mattresses onto the bed. Then the queen had twenty feather quilts piled on top of the twenty mattresses!

"Now we shall see if you are a real princess!" murmured the queen to herself.

The queen showed the princess to her room and tucked her into the towering bed. "Sleep well, my dear," she said.

In the morning the princess came down to breakfast, rubbing her eyes.

"How did you sleep, my dear?" the queen asked her.

The princess didn't want to be rude, but she couldn't lie. "I'm afraid I hardly slept a wink!" she replied, stifling a yawn.

"I'm so sorry, my dear," said the queen. "Was the bed not comfortable?"

"There were so many lovely mattresses and quilts, it should have been very comfortable," replied the princess, "but I could feel something lumpy and bumpy, and now I am black and blue all over!"

The queen grinned and hugged the girl to her. "That proves it," cried the queen. "Only a real princess would be able to feel a tiny pea through twenty mattresses and twenty feather quilts!"

The prince was filled with joy. He had finally met the princess of his dreams!

Not long after that, the prince asked Princess Penelope to be his wife. She happily agreed and they were married in the castle.

The prince was never unhappy again. And as for the pea, it was put in the royal museum as proof that perfect princesses do exist!

The End

Chicken Licken

One day, Chicken Licken was walking along when an acorn fell from a tree and bounced off his head. The acorn rolled away before Chicken Licken knew what had hit him.

"Oh, my! Oh, dear!" he clucked. "My goodness me, whatever shall I do?"

Chicken Licken flew into a panic. He ran around in circles in a flap, losing feathers as he went.

Along came Henny Penny.

"What's the matter?" she asked.

"THE SKY IS FALLING! THE SKY IS FALLING!" cried Chicken Licken, still in a panic.

Henny Penny was shocked. She did not know such a thing could happen.

"Cluck-a-cluck-cluck!" she shrieked. "We must tell the king at once!"

So Chicken Licken and Henny Penny rushed off to tell the king.

They flapped down the road, clucking as they went. Soon they met Cocky Locky.

"Where are you going in such a hurry?" he asked.

"THE SKY IS FALLING! THE SKY IS FALLING!" cried Chicken Licken.

"We're off to tell the king!" chattered Henny Penny.

Cocky Locky gasped. It would be terrible if the sky fell.

"Cock-a-doodle-doo," crowed Cocky Locky. "I'll come with you!"

So Chicken Licken, Henny Penny and Cocky Locky rushed off to tell the king.

They flapped and they flustered down the road, clucking and crowing as they went. Soon they met Ducky Lucky.

"Why are you flapping so?" she asked.

"THE SKY IS FALLING! THE SKY IS FALLING!" cried Chicken Licken.

"We're off to tell the king!" crowed Cocky Locky.

Ducky Lucky frowned. She didn't like the sound of that.

"How w-w-worrying," she quacked nervously. "I'm c-c-coming with you."

So Chicken Licken, Henny Penny, Cocky Locky and Ducky Lucky rushed off to tell the king.

They flapped and they flustered and they fidgeted down the road, clucking and crowing and quacking as they went. Soon they met Drakey Lakey.

"What's all the fuss about?" he asked.

"THE SKY IS FALLING! THE SKY IS FALLING!" cried Chicken Licken.

"We're off to tell the king!" quacked Ducky Lucky.

Drakey Lakey was dumbfounded. He dreaded the thought of a falling sky.

"Darn it!" he squawked. "I'll join you on your journey!"

So Chicken Licken, Henny Penny, Cocky Locky, Ducky Lucky and Drakey Lakey rushed off to tell the king.

They flapped and they flustered and they fidgeted and they flurried down the road, clucking and crowing and quacking and squawking as they went. Soon they met Goosey Loosey.

"What's ruffled your feathers?" she asked.

"THE SKY IS FALLING! THE SKY IS FALLING!" cried Chicken Licken.

"We're off to tell the king!" squawked Drakey Lakey.

Goosey Loosey shuddered. Could it really be true?

"How horrible!" she honked. "I'm coming with you."

So Chicken Licken, Henny Penny, Cocky Locky, Ducky Lucky, Drakey Lakey and Goosey Loosey rushed off to tell the king.

They flapped and they flustered and they fidgeted and they flurried and they flopped down the road, clucking and crowing and quacking and squawking and honking as they went. Soon they met Turkey Lurkey.

"Where are you waddling to?" she asked.

"THE SKY IS FALLING! THE SKY IS FALLING!" cried Chicken Licken.

"We're off to tell the king!" honked Goosey Loosey.

Turkey Lurkey trembled. She thought that sounded truly terrible!

"My goodness!" she gobbled. "I'm coming with you!"

So Chicken Licken, Henny Penny, Cocky Locky, Ducky Lucky, Drakey Lakey, Goosey Loosey and Turkey Lurkey rushed off to tell the king.

They flapped and they flustered and they fidgeted and they flurried and they flopped and they floundered down the road, clucking and crowing and quacking and squawking and honking and gobbling as they went. Soon they met Foxy Loxy.

"Well, hello!" he said. "Why are you all in such a tizzy?"

"THE SKY IS FALLING! THE SKY IS FALLING!" cried Chicken Licken.

"We're off to tell the king!" gobbled Turkey Lurkey.

Foxy Loxy smiled slyly. He had never seen so many plump birds in such a fearsome flap.

"Well I never," soothed Foxy Loxy. "Don't worry, I know the quickest way to reach the king. Follow me."

So Chicken Licken, Henny Penny, Cocky Locky, Ducky Lucky, Drakey Lakey, Goosey Loosey and Turkey Lurkey followed Foxy Loxy down a long path and into some dark woods.

"Not far to go now," said Foxy Loxy.

They lumbered over logs and they lolloped over leaves until they found themselves at... Foxy Loxy's den!

Foxy Loxy and all his family licked their lips.

"Run!" cried Chicken Licken.

"Fly!" shrieked Henny Penny.

"Hurry!" honked Goosey Loosey.

And Chicken Licken, Henny Penny, Cocky Locky, Ducky Lucky, Drakey Lakey, Goosey Loosey and Turkey Lurkey ran as fast as their legs could carry them.

They flapped and they flustered and they fidgeted and they flurried and they flopped and they floundered right out of the woods and back up the long path, clucking and crowing and quacking and squawking and honking and gobbling as they went.

And they never did tell the king about the sky falling.

The End

The Boy Who Cried Wolf

Once upon a time, there was a boy called Peter who lived in a little village in the mountains with his parents, who were sheep farmers. It was Peter's job to watch over the flock and protect the sheep from wolves.

Day after day, Peter sat on the mountainside watching the flock. It was very quiet with no one but sheep for company. No wolves ever came to eat the sheep.

Peter got very bored. He tried to amuse himself by climbing rocks and trees or by crawling through the grass and counting the sheep, one by one.

"One, two, three... sixty-four, sixty-five..." counted Peter, "Oh, I wish something exciting would happen. I'm so bored! Same old mountain, same old sheep..."

Finally, one day, Peter couldn't stand being bored any more.

"I know what to do!" he grinned to himself.

He started shouting at the top of his voice, "Wolf! Help! Wolf!"

Down in the village, a man heard Peter's cries.

"Quick!" he shouted to some other men. "We need to help Peter. There's a big wolf attacking the sheep."

The villagers grabbed their axes, forks, shovels and brooms and ran up the mountain to where Peter was shepherding his flock.

When they got there, puffing and panting, all was quiet and the sheep were grazing peacefully.

"Where's the wolf?" one of the villagers cried.

Peter roared with laughter. "There's no wolf. I was just playing!"

The men were very angry with Peter. "You mustn't cry wolf when there isn't one," they said.

That night Peter got a telling-off from his mother and was sent to bed without any supper.

For a while after this, Peter managed to behave himself. He climbed the mountainside with the sheep every day and watched over them quietly. The villagers soon forgot about his trick.

Then one day, Peter got really bored again. He had already run up and down the rocks, climbed three trees and counted the sheep ten times.

"What can I do now? Same old mountain, same old sheep..." he groaned to himself.

With a sigh, he slumped to the ground. As he was sitting there, an idea popped into his head. He picked up some sticks lying nearby and started banging them hard together. Then at the top of his voice, he shouted, "Wolf! Help! Wolf! Please hurry, there's a big wolf eating the sheep!"

Down in the village, a crowd of people started gathering when they heard the loud banging and shouting coming from the mountainside.

"What's all that noise?" someone cried.

"It's Peter. He's in trouble!" shouted someone else. "Quick, there must be a wolf on the prowl."

Once again, the villagers grabbed their forks, shovels and brooms. They ran up the mountain to chase away the wolf and save poor Peter and his sheep.

And once again, when they got there, puffing and out of breath, all was quiet and the sheep were grazing peacefully.

"Peter, what's happened?" shouted one man angrily.

"There's no wolf," laughed Peter. "I was only playing."

"You shouldn't make jokes like that," said another man. "It's not good to lie." The villagers marched back down the mountain towards the village.

That night, Peter got an even bigger telling-off from his mother and once again had to go to bed without any supper.

For a few days, the villagers went around moaning about Peter and his tricks. But after a while the incident was forgotten, and Peter continued to climb the mountainside every day with the sheep.

He had decided that he would try and behave himself, especially as he didn't want another scolding from his mother.

A few weeks later, while Peter stood counting the sheep as usual to pass the time, he noticed that some of them were bleating nervously. He climbed up a tree to take a look around and see what was upsetting them.

To his horror, he saw a big hairy wolf. The terrifying creature was creeping through the grass towards the flock with its jaws open and its long tongue hanging out. Peter could see the wolf's sharp pointed teeth.

Shaking with fear he started screaming, "Wolf! Help! Wolf! Please hurry, there's a big wolf about to eat the sheep!"

A few people down in the village heard his cries for help, but they carried on about their business as usual. "It's only Peter playing another trick," they said to each other. "Does he think he can fool us again?"

And so nobody went to Peter's rescue.

By nightfall, when Peter hadn't returned, his parents became concerned. Peter never missed his supper – something bad must have happened.

Peter's father gathered the people of the village, and together they hurried up the mountain, carrying flaming torches.

A terrible sight met their eyes. All the sheep were gone! There really had been a wolf this time.

Peter was still in the tree, shaking and crying.

"I cried out wolf! Why didn't you come?" he wept.

"Nobody believes a liar, even when he's speaking the truth," said Peter's father, helping him climb out of the tree. Peter hung on to his father all the way home. He never wanted to see another wolf ever again.

And Peter finally really learnt his lesson. He never told a lie again, and he always got to eat his dinner.

The End

Snow White

Once there was a queen who longed for a daughter. As she sat sewing by her window one winter's day, she pricked her finger on the needle. Three drops of blood fell from her finger, and she thought, "I wish I could have a daughter with lips as red as blood, hair as black as the ebony of this window-frame and skin as white as the snow outside."

Before long she gave birth to a beautiful baby daughter with blood-red lips, ebony hair and skin as white as snow.

"I will call you Snow White," whispered the queen to her new baby.

But soon after, the queen died and the king married again. His new bride was very beautiful, but also very vain. She had a magic mirror and every day she would look into it and ask:

"Mirror, mirror, on the wall,
Who is the fairest of them all?"

And the mirror would reply:

"You, O Queen,
are the fairest of them all."

As Snow White became more beautiful with every day that passed, her stepmother became more and more jealous. One day she asked the mirror:

"Mirror, mirror, on the wall,
Who is the fairest of them all?"

And the mirror replied:

"You, O Queen, are fair, it's true,
But young Snow White
is fairer than you."

When the queen heard these words she was furious. She called for her huntsman.

"Take Snow White into the forest and kill her!" she commanded.

The huntsman had to obey his queen. He led the beautiful girl deep into the forest. When he pulled out his knife, Snow White was very afraid and started to cry.

"Please, don't hurt me," she begged.

The huntsman took pity on her and decided to let her go.

"You must run as far from here as you can," he told her.

Snow White fled into the forest.

As darkness began to fall, Snow White came upon a little cottage. She knocked softly on the door, but there was no answer. She was so tired and frightened that she went inside anyway. There she found a table laid with seven places and a bedroom with seven little beds. Snow White lay down on the seventh bed and fell fast asleep.

She awoke to find seven little men all staring at her in amazement.

"Who are you?" she asked.

"We are the seven dwarves who live here," said one of the little men. "We work in the mines all day. Who are you?"

"I am Snow White," she replied.

When she told the dwarves her story, they were horrified.

"You can stay here with us," said the eldest dwarf.

So every day, the seven dwarves went off to work and Snow White stayed at the cottage and cooked and cleaned for them.

"Do not open the door to anyone," they told her as they left each morning, worried that the wicked queen would try to find her.

Meanwhile, the wicked queen asked her mirror:

"Mirror, mirror, on the wall,
Who is the fairest of them all?"

And the mirror replied:

"You, O Queen, are fair, it's true,
But Snow White is still fairer than you.
Deep in the forest with seven little men,
Snow White is living in a cosy den."

The wicked queen was furious and vowed that she would kill Snow White herself. She added poison to a juicy apple then disguised herself as a pedlar woman and set off into the forest.

"Who will buy my fresh apples?" she called out as she knocked at the door of the dwarves' cottage. Snow White loved apples, but remembered that she must not open the door to anyone. Instead, she opened the window to take a look. When the pedlar woman offered her an apple, she was nervous.

"There's no need to be frightened," said the disguised queen. She placed the apple in Snow White's hand. Snow White hesitated, then took a bite. The poison worked the moment it touched Snow White's beautiful red lips. The piece of apple became stuck in her throat and she fell down to the ground.

When the seven dwarves returned that evening, they were heartbroken to find that their beloved Snow White was dead. Such was their grief that they could not bear to bury her. The dwarves made a glass coffin for Snow White and placed it in the forest, where they took turns watching over it.

One day, a prince rode by.

"Who is this beautiful girl?" asked the prince.

The dwarves told the prince Snow White's sad story and the prince wept.

"Please let me take her away," begged the prince. "I promise I will watch over her."

The dwarves could see how much the prince loved Snow White, so they agreed to let her go.

As the prince's servants lifted the coffin, they lost their grip. The fall jolted the piece of poisoned apple from Snow White's throat and she came back to life.

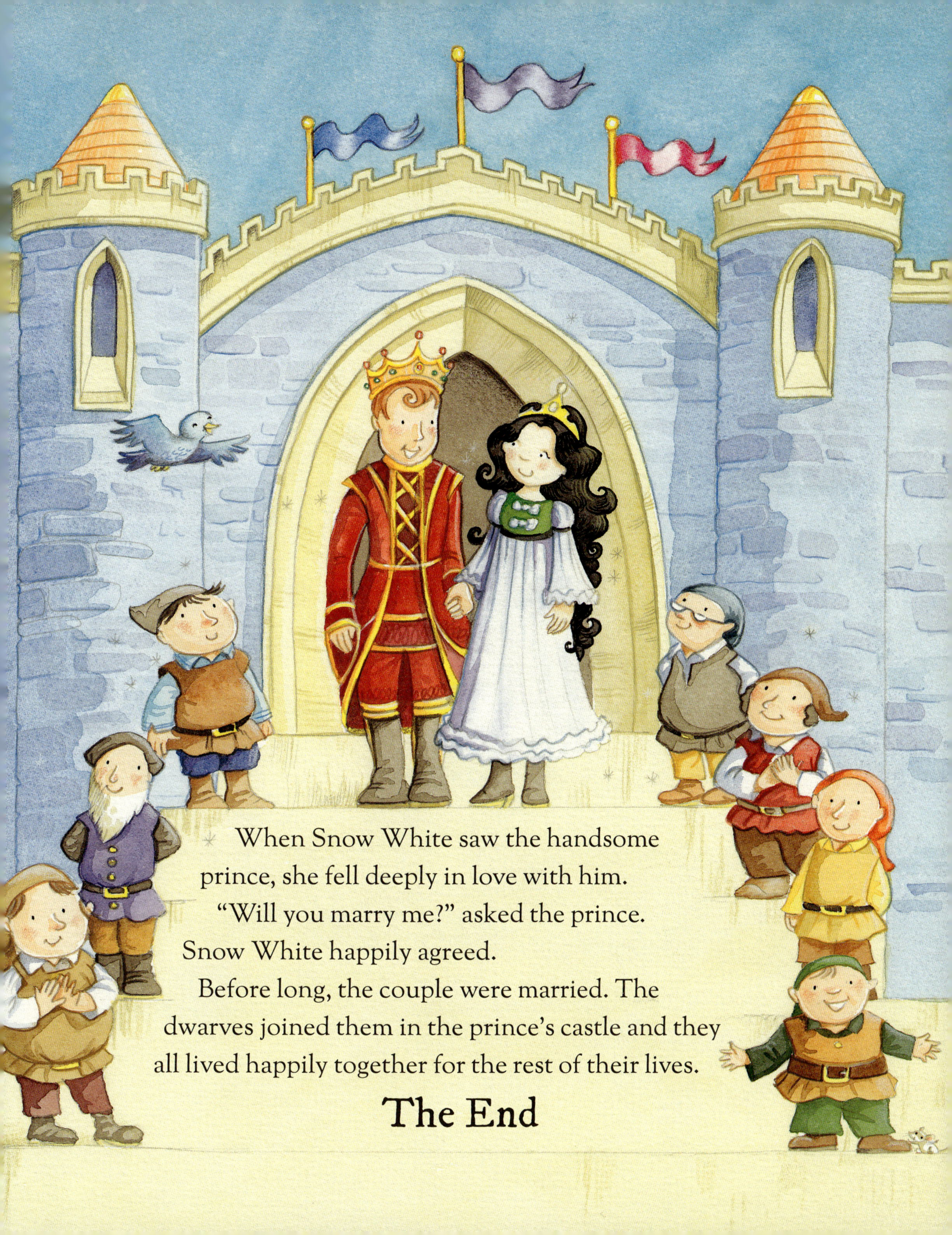

When Snow White saw the handsome prince, she fell deeply in love with him.

"Will you marry me?" asked the prince. Snow White happily agreed.

Before long, the couple were married. The dwarves joined them in the prince's castle and they all lived happily together for the rest of their lives.

The End

Jack and the Beanstalk

Once upon a time, there was a young boy called Jack, who lived with his mother in a cottage. They were so poor that, bit by bit, they had to sell everything they owned just to buy their food. Then one day, Jack's mother said to him,

"We will have to sell Bluebell, our old cow. Take her to the market, Jack, and remember to sell her for a good price."

So Jack took Bluebell off to market. He had just reached the edge of the town when an old man appeared at the side of the road.

"Are you going to sell that fine cow?" said the man.

"Yes," said Jack.

"Well, I'll buy her from you, and I'll give you these magic beans," said the man, holding out a handful of dry beans. "They don't look much, but if you plant them, you and your mother will be rich beyond your wildest dreams."

Jack liked the sound of being rich. And he didn't even stop to wonder how this stranger knew about his mother!

"It's a deal!" he said. He gave Bluebell to the man and took the beans.

When Jack showed his mother the beans, she was so angry that her face turned as red as a beetroot!

"You stupid boy! Go to your room!" she cried, and threw the beans out of the window.

Jack sat on his bed, feeling miserable. "Stupid beans," he muttered. "Stupid me!" Then he fell asleep.

When Jack woke up the next morning, it was strangely dark in his room and all he could see through the window were the leaves of a huge plant. A plant so tall that he couldn't see the top of it.

"It must be a magic beanstalk!" cried Jack. "What's at the top?"

So Jack started to climb. Up he went, from branch to branch and from leaf to leaf. At the top was a giant house. Jack's tummy was rumbling with hunger, so he knocked on the great big door. A giant woman answered.

"Please, madam, may I have some breakfast?" Jack asked politely.

"You'll become breakfast if my husband finds you!" said the giant's wife. But Jack begged and pleaded and at last she let him in and gave him some bread and milk.

The giant's wife had just shown Jack where to hide when the giant came home in a bad mood.

"Fee, fi, fo, fum, I smell the blood of an Englishman!" roared the giant.

"Silly man," said his wife. "You smell the sausages I have cooked you for breakfast."

The giant ate a giant-sized breakfast, then settled down to count the huge gold coins in his treasure chest. There were lots of coins. "One hundred and one... one hundred and two..." he counted, but his head started to nod and before long he was fast asleep.

Quick as a flash, Jack grabbed two of the huge gold coins and ran out through the front door. He raced to the beanstalk and climbed down it as fast as his legs would carry him.

His mother was so happy to see the gold that she hugged Jack for ten whole minutes!

"Clever boy, Jack!" she laughed. "We'll never be poor again!"

Before long, however, Jack and his mother had spent all the money, so the boy decided to climb the beanstalk again. Just as before, Jack knocked on the door and asked the giant's wife for some food. He begged and he pleaded and at last she let him in. She gave him some bread and milk and hid him in the cupboard just as the giant arrived home.

When the giant had eaten a giant-sized lunch, his wife brought him his pet hen. "Lay!" he bellowed, and the hen laid a solid gold egg. It laid ten eggs before the giant started to snore. Jack could hardly believe his luck! Quick as a flash, he picked up the hen and ran.

When his mother saw the hen lay a golden egg, she hugged Jack for twenty whole minutes!

Although Jack and his mother were now rich beyond their wildest dreams, the boy couldn't help himself – he decided to climb the beanstalk one more time.

This time, Jack knew that the giant's wife would not be happy to see him, so he sneaked in when she wasn't looking and quickly hid in the cupboard. The giant came home as usual and ate a giant-sized dinner, then his wife brought him his magic harp.

"Play!" he roared, and the harp began to play. It was such sweet music that the giant fell asleep in record time!

Jack grabbed the harp and started to run, but the harp cried out, "Master! Help!"

The giant woke up at once and chased after Jack. The boy slithered down the beanstalk faster than he'd ever done before, but the giant was catching up!

"Mother, fetch me the axe!" Jack yelled as he reached the ground. Then he chopped at the beanstalk with all his might. **Creak! Groan!** The giant quickly climbed back up to the top just before the beanstalk crashed to the ground.

When his mother heard the harp play, she hugged Jack for a whole hour! And, as you can imagine, the two of them lived happily ever after.

The End

The Emperor's New Clothes

Once upon a time, there lived an emperor who really loved clothes. He would strut around his palace in different outfits, day and night. There were mirrors in every room so he could admire his reflection as he passed by.

The emperor had outfits for the morning...

...and different outfits for the afternoon...

...and extra special outfits for the evening made from the most expensive cloth and sewn with pure gold thread.

In fact, the emperor had so many clothes that he often didn't know what to wear!

One day, two wicked men called at the palace. They knew all about the emperor's love of clothes.

"Your Highness, we are weavers," they said. "But we can do something that no other weavers can do. We can make a magic cloth. This cloth is very special because only very clever people can see it."

The emperor was impressed. "I would like you to make me a suit from this magic cloth," he said.

"Of course, Your Highness, it would be an honour," said the first weaver.

"Sire, we will need lots of gold thread," said the second weaver.

"You shall have all the gold thread you need," replied the emperor. He turned to one of his servants. "Please show these fine gentlemen to the royal storeroom."

The two men had never seen so much gold thread. Laughing and clapping their hands with glee, they filled their bags, and left the palace.

A few days later the emperor called for one of his ministers.

"Go and find out how the weavers are getting on," he ordered impatiently. "I need something new to wear."

The minister went off to the weavers' workshop. There he found the two weavers sitting in front of a loom, busy at work.

The minister rubbed his eyes. He couldn't see any cloth on the loom.

"That's strange," he thought. Not wanting to appear foolish, he smiled at the weavers.

"The cloth is looking wonderful. When will the emperor's suit be ready?" he asked.

"Soon, soon," replied the first weaver.

"But we will need more gold thread to complete the suit," said the second weaver.

The minister hurried back to the emperor. As soon as he had gone, the weavers roared with laughter.

"Oh, this is priceless! What a foolish man!"

Back at the palace, the minister bowed before the emperor. Not wishing to be called a fool he said, "Sire, I have never seen a cloth more beautiful. The weavers need more gold thread to finish your suit."

"Well, send more over then," replied the emperor.

For a whole week the weavers pretended to cut and sew the magic cloth to make the new suit. At last they returned to the palace, proudly pretending to carry the cloth.

The emperor was very excited and handed the weavers a bag of gold coins to pay for the outfit. He took off his clothes and the weavers fussed around him, pretending to smooth and adjust the suit.

"It fits you perfectly!" they cried.

The emperor looked in the mirror. He couldn't see any clothes, but not wanting to appear foolish, he said, "It's wonderful!"

As soon as the two men had left the palace, they doubled over with laughter. Their cunning plan had worked.

News of the emperor's suit quickly spread throughout the kingdom. Everyone was sure they would be able to see the magic cloth.

The vain emperor sent out a royal announcement. He would lead a grand procession through the city wearing his new suit.

When the great day arrived, the emperor sent for the two weavers to help him get dressed.

"Ah, Your Highness, you do look wonderful," they cried.

"Yes, Sire, truly splendid!" agreed the emperor's ministers.

No matter how hard he looked, the emperor still could not see any clothes.

"I can't be more of a fool than my ministers," he thought, "and they can all see the suit." So he smiled at the weavers and thanked them once again.

People had gathered in the streets to catch a glimpse of the emperor as the procession passed by. Finally the emperor appeared riding on a fine white horse. Nervous whispers rippled through the crowd. No one wanted to appear foolish, so at last a timid voice called out;

"The emperor's new clothes are magnificent!"

Suddenly everyone started talking and shouting at once.

"How stylish!"

"Smart and fashionable!"

The emperor smiled as he trotted along, feeling very pleased with himself. Then a small boy and his sister pushed to the front of the crowd. They started to point and giggle.

"Look!" they cried. "The emperor has no clothes on!"

Suddenly, everyone knew that it was true. Before long the laughter had spread through the crowd.

The emperor turned bright red. "What a fool I am!" he gasped. "How could I have been so silly and vain?" He looked around for the two weavers, but of course they were nowhere to be seen.

Filled with shame, the emperor made his way back to the palace to get dressed.

"I will never be so vain about my clothes again," said the emperor to his minister.

He was true to his word – and he was a much happier emperor from that day on.

The End

The Little Mermaid

Long, long ago, a mer-king lived under the sea with his six mermaid daughters, who all had long wavy hair and sang with sweet heavenly voices.

The mermaids loved their watery world, but they liked to hear the wise sea king tell them stories about the world above the sea.

"Oh, father, tell us about the cities and the trees and flowers!" they would cry.

"When you are twenty-one, my little ones," their father would say, "you can go to the surface and see all these wonders for yourself."

One by one, the sisters got their chance to visit the surface. At last it was the turn of the youngest sister. The little mermaid swam up through the crystal waters to the ocean surface with great joy in her heart.

Close by was a big ship. She could see people on the deck throwing a party for the prince who was on board.

The little mermaid couldn't keep her eyes off the handsome prince. As she swam closer for a better look, the sea started to swell and a strong wind whipped up.

"Oh no!" cried the little mermaid. "A storm is coming."

Suddenly, as the ship was tossed from side to side, the prince was thrown into the churning water. He began to sink beneath the waves and would have drowned had the little mermaid not dived down to rescue him.

Swimming close to the land, she gently pushed the unconscious prince onto the beach. His eyes flickered open for a few seconds and he smiled before closing them again. As she swam away, she glanced back at the shore. A group of people had gathered around the prince. They helped him to his feet and led him away down the beach.

The little mermaid dived beneath the waves and swam back home.

The little mermaid longed to see the prince again. She became so sad that eventually she told her sisters about the prince and how she had fallen in love with him.

"I know where his palace is," said her oldest sister. "I'll show you."

After that, the little mermaid swam to the surface every day. She gazed at the palace hoping to catch a glimpse of the prince.

"Father, could I become human, if I wanted to?" she asked the king one day.

"The only way, my little one," said the king gently, "is if a human falls in love with you."

But the little mermaid could not forget the prince. She decided to visit the sea witch.

"I can make a potion to make you human," hissed the witch. "But I will take your beautiful voice as my payment. If you win the true love of the prince, only then will you get your voice back."

The little mermaid loved the prince so much that she agreed. She swam to the prince's palace and drank the potion. She fell into a deep sleep.

When she woke up, she was lying on the beach dressed in beautiful clothes. Where her shiny tail had been, she now had a pair of pale human legs. The little mermaid tried to stand, but her new legs wobbled and she stumbled on the sand.

As she fell, two strong arms reached out and caught her. The little mermaid looked up. It was the prince! She tried to speak but her voice had gone, and she could only smile at her handsome rescuer.

The silent, beautiful and mysterious stranger fascinated the prince. He grew very fond of the little mermaid and spent his afternoons with her around the palace.

One day, the prince told the little mermaid that he was getting married to a princess.

"My parents want me to do this," he sighed sadly. "But I love another girl. I don't know who she is, but she once rescued me from the sea."

The little mermaid was devastated, but without a voice, how could she tell the prince that she was that girl?

A few days before the wedding, the prince asked the little mermaid to take a walk with him along the beach.

"Once I'm married, I won't be able to spend so much time with you," he told her.

The little mermaid nodded sadly. She had been dreading this happening.

As they walked across the sand, a fierce wind suddenly whipped along the shore. A huge wave crashed over the prince and the little mermaid, washing them out to sea. Without thinking, the little mermaid dived beneath the churning waves and grabbed the prince.

As the prince lay coughing and spluttering on the sand, he stared at the little mermaid.

"You're the girl who saved me before!" he cried. "I remember now."

The little mermaid smiled and nodded.

"I can't marry the princess. I love you," he sighed. "I don't care if you can't speak. Will you marry me?"

The little mermaid had never felt so joyful and, as the prince kissed her, something magical happened. She could feel her voice returning! Bubbling with excitement, she cried out, "Yes, I will marry you!"

The happy couple were married the very next day. The little mermaid's dreams had come true, but she never forgot her family, or that she had once been a mermaid.

The End

The Sorcerer's Apprentice

Once upon a time, a young boy called Franz went to work as an apprentice for a sorcerer. The sorcerer lived in a huge castle overlooking the little village where Franz lived with his family. It was considered a great honour to help and learn from such a clever and powerful man.

Franz was very excited about learning how to do magic. But when he arrived on his first day, he was just given a long list of chores to do around the castle – cleaning, tidying up and fetching water from the well.

Franz was not happy. "It's not fair!" he muttered to himself. "I didn't come here to be his servant. When will I get to do some magic?"

The sorcerer was a busy man. Each morning he would tell his apprentice what chores needed doing that day. He would then disappear into his workshop in the castle or journey out to one of the surrounding villages in the area, leaving Franz alone.

Occasionally, as Franz went about the castle doing his chores, he would catch a glimpse of the great sorcerer looking through the pages of a large leather-bound book, which he kept locked in a wooden cabinet in his workshop. The pages of this book were filled with beautiful illustrations and the words of the sorcerer's magic spells. Franz longed to have a look in the book himself.

Several months later, fed up with just doing chores all day, Franz decided he would sneak a look in the sorcerer's special spell book when the old man was gone.

As the sorcerer got ready to leave the castle that day, he called out to Franz.

"Boy, I need you to scrub the floor of the Great Hall for me," he said. "You will need to fetch water from the well with this bucket, and carry it to the big stone container in the hall."

Franz rolled his eyes behind the sorcerer's back. "Of course, sir," he mumbled.

"When the container is full of water," continued the sorcerer, "take the broom and give the floor a good scrub. I want to see it shining when I get back this afternoon."

As soon as the sorcerer left, Franz climbed the small staircase to the workshop. He knew where the sorcerer kept the key to the wooden cabinet, so he grabbed it and hurriedly opened the old, creaking doors. Inside, on a shelf, sat the magic spell book.

Franz carried the heavy book to the Great Hall and sat down to look through its magical pages. There were spells for all sorts of weird and wonderful things.

As he turned the pages, Franz saw a spell that could bring any object to life. This gave him a brilliant idea.

"What harm can one little spell do?" he thought to himself.

Grinning, Franz rushed to fetch the broom and bucket. He placed the broom on the floor, sat back down at the desk and slowly chanted the words of the magic spell. He couldn't wait to see the broom clean the Great Hall by itself!

At first nothing happened. Franz was just about to try the spell again, when suddenly the broom sprouted little arms and leapt up from the floor. Franz was so surprised he nearly fell off his chair!

This was amazing. He was doing magic!

"Broom!" he commanded. "Take the bucket to the well and fetch water to fill that container."

The broom marched off to the well and started carrying the bucket backwards and forwards between the well and the container in the Great Hall.

Franz couldn't believe his eyes. Laughing as the little broom kept bringing the water, he cried, "I am the master! And you must obey me!"

After a while, Franz noticed that the container was overflowing and that the water was running all over the floor.

"Stop, little broom!" he shouted. The broom, however, carried on fetching water.

"What am I to do now?" thought Franz. Flipping through the pages of the magic book, he tried to find a spell to make the broom stop.

But the broom kept on going. By now the water was all over the floor. Franz grabbed an axe and chopped the broom into small pieces.

"That should do it," he said with a sigh of relief.

To his dismay, the little pieces of broom started to move and grow, and they too sprouted arms and legs. Soon there was an army of new brooms. They all began to march to the well to fetch more water.

Franz didn't know what to do! The brooms continued splashing the water into the Great Hall and soon it was swirling around Franz's knees. He was powerless to stop the brooms.

Just then, the sorcerer returned. He raised his arms and in a booming voice, chanted a magic spell. In an instant the brooms all vanished and the water disappeared. Everything returned to normal.

Shaking with fear, Franz fell to his knees. "Please forgive me, master," he begged. "I just wanted to try some magic."

The sorcerer was very angry. "Never play with things you don't understand!" he shouted. "Magic is very powerful and should only be used by a sorcerer."

Franz hung his head in shame. He would never get the chance to learn magic now.

"I should send you away, boy," continued the sorcerer, but he could see that Franz was very sorry. He decided to give him another chance.

"You can stay," he said. "You still have much training to complete."

Franz was so relieved. "Thank you, sir!" he said. "I promise I will work very hard."

"Well," said the sorcerer, "you can start by cleaning this floor – the old-fashioned way!"

The End

Little Red Riding Hood

There was once a sweet and happy little girl whose granny had made her a lovely red cape with a hood. The little girl loved it so much that she wore it everywhere she went. Soon everyone became so used to her wearing it that they called her 'Little Red Riding Hood'.

"Little Red Riding Hood," said her mother one morning, "Granny is not feeling very well. Take her this basket of food and see if you can cheer her up."

Little Red Riding Hood loved to visit her granny, so she took the basket of food and set off right away.

"Go straight to Granny's house and don't talk to any strangers!" her mother called after her.

"Don't worry," sang Little Red Riding Hood as she went merrily on her way.

Little Red Riding Hood skipped off through the wood. The sun was shining, the birds were chirping in the treetops and she didn't have a care in the world.

Very soon she met a wolf.

"Well, hello there," said the wolf in a silky, low voice. "And where are you off to on this fine morning?"

"I'm going to visit my granny," replied Little Red Riding Hood, forgetting her mother's warning. "She's feeling poorly and I'm taking her this food to make her better."

The wolf licked his lips.

"Where does your dear old granny live?" asked the wolf.

"She lives in a cottage at the other side of the wood," replied Little Red Riding Hood. "It has pretty roses growing around the door."

"Is that so?" said the wolf. "Why, it sounds lovely!"

There were some beautiful wild flowers growing in the wood and Little Red Riding Hood stopped to admire them.

"Why don't you pick a pretty posy for your granny?" suggested the wolf.

Little Red Riding Hood thought that was a good idea and stooped down to pick some. As she was busy choosing the prettiest flowers, the wolf strolled away down the path. His tummy rumbled loudly. At the end of the path, he saw a cottage with roses growing around the door, just as Little Red Riding Hood had said.

The wicked old wolf knocked on the door. "Come right in, my darling," called the grandmother, thinking that it was Little Red Riding Hood.

The wolf walked into the cottage. Before the grandmother had a chance to call for help the wicked creature opened his huge jaws and swallowed her whole! Then he climbed into her bed, pulled the covers up under his chin and waited.

Soon, Little Red Riding Hood reached her granny's house with her basket of food and a beautiful bunch of wild flowers.

"Won't granny be pleased to see me!" she thought, as she knocked on the door.

"Come right in, my darling," replied a strange, croaky voice.

"Poor Granny," thought Little Red Riding Hood. "She doesn't sound at all well!"

Little Red Riding Hood looked in the kitchen, but her granny wasn't there. She looked in the sitting room, but her granny wasn't there either. Finally she went into her granny's bedroom, and she gasped in surprise.

"Granny," exclaimed Little Red Riding Hood. "Your ears are absolutely enormous!"

"All the better to hear you with, my dear," replied a low, silky voice.

"And your eyes are as big as saucers," gulped Little Red Riding Hood.

"All the better to see you with," replied a rumbling, growly voice.

"And your teeth are so... pointed!" gasped Little Red Riding Hood.

"All the better to EAT you with!" snarled a loud, hungry voice.

The wicked old wolf leaped out of bed and gobbled up Little Red Riding Hood in one big GULP! Then he lay down on the bed and fell fast asleep.

Luckily, a woodcutter was working nearby, and he heard some very loud and growly snoring sounds coming from the little cottage.

"I don't like the sound of that!" he thought. With his axe at the ready he crept into the grandmother's house. He tiptoed into the bedroom and found the wolf fast asleep... with his tummy bulging fit to burst!

"You wicked old wolf!" cried the woodcutter. "What have you done?"

He tipped the wolf upside-down and shook him as hard as he could. Out fell a very dazed Little Red Riding Hood, followed by her poor old granny.

"It was so dark in there!" cried the little girl. "Thank you for saving us!"

But Little Red Riding Hood's granny was FURIOUS! She chased the wolf out of her bedroom, through the cottage and out into the wood. The woodcutter and Little Red Riding Hood followed close behind her.

The wolf never returned, and Little Red Riding Hood never spoke to strangers ever again.

The End